the

INCORRIGIBLE CHILDREN
of
ASHTON PLACE

Book 1: THE MYSTERIOUS HOWLING

by **MARYROSE WOOD**
illustrated by **JON KLASSEN**

BALZER + BRAY
An Imprint of HarperCollins*Publishers*

Balzer + Bray is an imprint of HarperCollins Publishers.

The Incorrigible Children of Ashton Place Book 1: The Mysterious Howling
Text copyright © 2010 by Maryrose Wood Illustrations copyright © 2010 by Jon Klassen

Library of Congress Cataloging-in-Publication Data.
Wood, Maryrose.
   The mysterious howling / by Maryrose Wood ; illustrated by Jon Klassen. — 1st ed.
      p.   cm. — (The incorrigible children of Ashton Place ; bk. 1)
   Summary: Fifteen-year-old Miss Penelope Lumley, a recent graduate of the Swanburne
Academy for Poor Bright Females, is hired as governess to three young children who have
been raised by wolves and must teach them to behave in a civilized manner quickly, in
preparation for a Christmas ball.
   ISBN 978-0-06-179105-5
   [1. Governesses—Fiction. 2. Feral children—Fiction. 3. Orphans—Fiction. 4. Balls
(Parties)—Fiction. 5. Christmas—Fiction.] I. Klassen, J., ill. II. Title.
PZ7.W8524Mys 2010   2009024256
   [Fic]—dc22

Typography by Sarah Hoy
10 11 12 13 14   CG/RRDB   10 9 8 7 6 5 4 3 2
❖
First Edition

For Mike
—M.W.

THE FIRST CHAPTER

One home is forsaken in hopes
of finding another.

IT WAS NOT MISS PENELOPE LUMLEY'S first journey on a train, but it was the first one she had taken alone.

As you may know, traveling alone is quite a different kettle of fish from traveling with companions. It tends to make people anxious, especially when en route to a strange place, or a new home, or a job interview, or (as in the case of Miss Lumley) a job interview in a strange place that might very well end up being her new home.

She certainly had much to be anxious about. During

the journey her worried thoughts had included the following:

Would she arrive at Ashton Place on time for her interview, or would masked bandits storm the train and take the passengers hostage? She had never personally encountered a bandit, but she had read of such things in books, and the very idea gave her goose bumps.

Would she be able to answer correctly should her prospective employers quiz her on, say, the capital cities of midsized European nations? "The capital of Hungary is Budapest!" she had recited in her mind, in time to the *clickity-clack* of the train wheels. "The capital of Poland is Warsaw!"

Would she be served tea and toast upon her arrival, and if she were, would she end up with marmalade all over the front of her dress and run from the room weeping?

Clearly, being anxious is a full-time and rather exhausting occupation. Perhaps that explains why Miss Lumley, despite her inability to remember the capital of Norway and her reluctance to muss her hair by leaning her head against the back of her seat, had finally succumbed to the soothing sway and rumble of the train. For the moment, at least, she had stopped worrying altogether, for she was soundly and deeply asleep.

To be more specific: She was lost in a dream of long ago, a dream filled with laughter and Black Forest cake and sun-dappled meadows that rang with the singing of adorable birds—

"Miss? Miss?" The conductor stood in the aisle next to her seat and spoke a bit louder than he normally would, in order to be heard over the screechy din of the train's brakes being applied.

"Is it the bandits?" Miss Lumley cried, half asleep. "For, though unarmed, I will fight!"

"There are no bandits, miss." The conductor looked rather embarrassed. "Forgive me for disturbing you, but we are arriving at Ashton Station. May I remove your luggage from the train?"

As a very wise woman (whom we shall soon hear more about) once declared, "There is no alarm clock like embarrassment," and by the time the conductor spoke the word *luggage*, Miss Lumley was far more awake than she wished to be. Had she really said something about bandits? She had seen cats fall clumsily from windowsills and then walk off as if nothing undignified had happened; this, Miss Lumley realized, was her wisest course of action. Best not to mention the bandits, ever again.

"You are forgiven," she said as she stood, "and you may."

She followed the conductor down the aisle, staggering from side to side as the train lurched to a stop. The scrubbed-looking youth blushed scarlet as he heaved her trunk and carpetbag onto the platform.

"I do apologize, miss!" He extended a hand to help her descend the steep metal stair. "It's only that I didn't want you to miss your stop—"

"And as you can see, I have not." She nodded her thanks and then shook her head, as if to say, "How ridiculous, *meow!* To think I would travel all this way only to miss my stop, *meow meow!*" But in the end she offered him a tiny smile, and this was enough to make the young man swell with pride at the fine service he had provided that day.

In fact, the competence and dedication of the young conductor would soon come to the attention of his superiors, who would waste no time offering the stalwart fellow a promotion. Over the years, he would work his way up through the ranks and eventually become Chief Locomotive Officer, a position that would render him modestly well-to-do and a perfectly well-liked chap to all who knew him.

But this happy ending, like so many others, was still far off in the future. For now, the conductor simply watched through the window as the train pulled away. He saw how the rapidly receding Miss Lumley stood unmoving among the great puffs of steam, the blood-curdling scream of the wheels singing high over the melancholy tenor of the train whistle and the deep bass roar of the engine. Like the conductor, at that moment Miss Lumley had no way of predicting whether her life would turn out happily or in some other, less desirable way.

Luckily, she knew better than to brood about such things. Although only fifteen years old, she was a recent graduate of the Swanburne Academy for Poor Bright Females. During her years at that well-regarded school, Miss Lumley had been taught a great deal, of both an academic and a philosophical nature. At the heart of her education were the sayings of Agatha Swanburne, the school's founder and a woman of unparalleled common sense (she was, as you have already guessed, the very wise woman previously mentioned). These pithy kernels of truth were not unlike those you might find inside the fortune cookies at a Chinese restaurant—although you can be sure that neither Agatha Swanburne nor Miss Lumley had ever set foot in such an establishment.

Agatha Swanburne, Miss Lumley felt quite sure, would not succumb to nervous fits simply because she was standing alone on a train platform in a strange town with all her meager worldly goods around her, wishing that she had never had to leave her beloved school to make her own way in the world. But it could not be helped. Miss Lumley had graduated (a year early and at the top of her class, it should be said), and there was no longer any room for her at the academy, "what with the constant influx of Poor Bright Females waiting for a spot to open up!" That is how Miss Charlotte Mortimer, the kind headmistress at Swanburne, had explained the situation.

"A person's life can certainly change a great deal in two days," Miss Lumley thought. And yet, she reminded herself, Agatha Swanburne would not waste a moment worrying about things that couldn't be helped, or events that hadn't happened yet, or subjects that were otherwise useless to dwell upon. Nor would she squeeze her own right hand tightly with her left, close her eyes and pretend, just for a moment, that it was Miss Charlotte Mortimer holding her hand and that, when she opened her eyes, she would be surrounded by familiar people and places, and everything in her life would remain as it had always been.

No, Agatha Swanburne would sit calmly upon her trunk to wait for her ride to Ashton Place, and perhaps take out a favorite volume of poetry to pass the time. And that is exactly what Miss Penelope Lumley did. She may have been young and alone, in a strange place with no real home to return to and on her way to a job interview, but she was also much, much more than her current circumstances would indicate.

She was a Swanburne girl, through and through.

ONE OF AGATHA SWANBURNE'S SAYINGS, which Penelope had often heard (you may think of her as Penelope from this point forward, for now you have made her acquaintance), was this: "All books are judged by their covers until they are read."

She had never understood the true meaning of this expression until now. Imagine: A studious-looking girl of fifteen, primly dressed, perched on a large, battered trunk and reading a well-thumbed volume of obscure poetry—what tableau could more perfectly match what any reasonable person might expect a young governess to look like?

It was, as they say nowadays, perfect casting. Doubtless that is why the coachman from Ashton Place took only a moment to recognize Penelope on the platform. In spite of her youth, he addressed her with all the deference due a professional educator. Nor did he offer any complaint at the alarming weight of the trunk.

"Full a' books, I take it?" He grunted as he hoisted it into the carriage. Then he held the door open for her to enter. Penelope hesitated.

"May I ride outside, next to you?" she asked. "The weather is so fine, and I am curious to see what the town of Ashton is like, in case I am asked to stay," she added, striking what she hoped was the right note of humility. Swanburne girls were encouraged to be confident and bold, but Miss Mortimer had also advised Penelope to show some restraint when meeting new people—"only until you get to know each other a bit," she explained. Penelope had always found Miss Mortimer's advice to be well worth taking.

"Hmph," the coachman said, but he helped Penelope climb up next to him in the driver's seat. Penelope noted the horses' gleaming coats with approval. Her soft spot for animals was well known at Swanburne—indeed, that is what had caught Miss Mortimer's eye in the advertisement for the position. Could it truly have been only a week since that fateful day? If Penelope closed her eyes, she could still hear Miss Mortimer's voice. . . .

"Listen to this, girls: 'Wanted *Immediately*: Energetic Governess for Three Lively Children.'" Miss Mortimer often shared breakfast with her favorites among the students and would read the newspaper aloud to them as they gobbled up their boiled oats and milk. "'Knowledge of French, Latin, History, Etiquette, Drawing, and Music will be Required—*Experience with Animals Strongly Preferred.*' Animals! Did you hear that? It is the perfect job for you, Penny, dear!" Her warm voice had throbbed with conviction as she handed Penelope the page torn from the latest edition of *Heathcote, All Year Round (Now Illustrated).* "No arguments! You must have an interview. I will write your recommendation at once."

Now that same sheet of newspaper was carefully folded and tucked inside Penelope's volume of poetry, serving as both bookmark and, she hoped, lucky charm. "It sounds as if the children are deeply attached to their pets," she told herself, as the horses *clip-clopp*ed along the road through the ancient forest that lay between the village and the estate, "and that means they are likely to be from a kind and fun-loving family, and we shall all get along splendidly."

The idea was so comforting, she almost asked the coachman what sort of animals she could expect to meet at Ashton Place. She dearly hoped there were ponies on the premises. Penelope had secretly wished for a pony ever since she was a tiny girl and discovered the Giddy-Yap, Rainbow! books in the Swanburne library. The adventures of Rainbow and her young mistress, Edith-Anne Pevington, had filled many a happy hour curled up on the window seat of Miss Mortimer's office. The volume titled *Silky Mischief*, in which Rainbow's gentle influence saves an ill-tempered pony on a neighboring farm from a gruesome fate, left an especially lasting impression. Penelope had reread it more times than she could count.

But upon reflection she felt it would be more polite to inquire about other topics first. She adjusted her bonnet and pulled her cloak around her against the early autumn breeze.

"Tell me, sir: What sort of a house is Ashton Place?"

"Very grand, as you'll soon see. Four generations of Ashtons have lived out their days there." The coachman paused and clucked encouragement to the horses and then went on. "I reckon it's lucky a house can't speak. If it could, Ashton Place could tell all manner a' secrets."

Penelope found his imagery quaint, if a tad unoriginal, but knew better than to say so. Instead, she asked, "And what sort of people are Lord and Lady Ashton? I know they are of the finest character, of course!"

"I don't imagine a proper young lady like you would have come for the interview otherwise," he said, giving her a sly, sideways look. Penelope wondered if she was being teased and decided that it was unlikely, since she and the coachman had just met. In any case, he proceeded to answer her question.

"Lady Constance is fond of chocolates and flowers. She's very young, very pretty, and a bit on the spoiled side, in my opinion."

"You speak quite freely of your employers," Penelope commented.

"Ha! I've the right to speak my mind. I've been working for the Ashtons since Lord Fredrick was a boy—whoa, whoa!"

Startled by the sudden rise of a flock of geese from the roadside, the horses had broken into a canter. The coachman quickly pulled them back to a steady trot.

"As for Lord Fredrick," the coachman continued, "he spends more time at his gentlemen's club than you'd expect of a newly married man, but to each his own, I say. For sport, he loves to hunt. Fox and deer, hares and badgers and all manner a' birds. On occasion he's bagged more . . . *unusual* prey."

It seemed to Penelope that a note of mystery briefly

entered his voice, but it disappeared just as quickly.

"Any other questions?"

Despite his gruffness, Penelope smiled. After sharing such a pleasant journey in the fresh air, she felt that she and coachman were now friends and could trust each other.

"Tell me about the children! I so look forward to meeting them."

"Ah," he said, his face suddenly clouding over. "The children are—well, I do think it's Lady Ashton's place to discuss the children, I do."

And, except for one brief and heartfelt outburst (which would not occur for another three-quarters of an hour), that was the last word he spoke for the rest of the journey.

THE SECOND CHAPTER

Penelope and Lady Constance
converse to the accompaniment
of strange noises.

IF YOU HAVE EVER VISITED a theme park full of roller coasters, water slides, and thrilling games of chance, you were undoubtedly tickled half to death by it all. But then, just when it seemed the excitement had reached a fever pitch from which you might never recover, the tedious ordeal of waiting in a long line for the bathroom may have suddenly made you so bored that you wished you were home in bed with the flu.

So it was with Penelope. Despite the two days of

anxious travel she had just endured and the important job interview that awaited her, as she sat there trapped in the carriage seat next to a coachman who had decided not to talk, Penelope grew excruciatingly bored. She decided it would be rude to glance at her poetry book.

"I shall have to resort to the scenery to keep me occupied," she thought, turning her mind to the task. They were now passing through stately woods. Dutifully she admired the golden-tipped canopy of leaves and observed how the sunlight could penetrate only here and there, dappling a lush undergrowth of ferns. Some of these she could identify even from a distance: Hart's-tongue ferns, cinnamon ferns, and some with attractive crinkled edges she thought were called corrugated ferns or, if they weren't, ought to be. Penelope had once attended a lecture at Swanburne given by the deputy vice president of the Heathcote Amateur Pteridological Society, and considered herself quite knowledgeable about ferns as a result.

Then she imagined the trees as they would soon look in the full blaze of autumn color—and then afterward, in winter, as a field of bare-branched giants standing on a blanket of white. It made her wonder (although not aloud), "And where will I be come Christmas? If all goes well, I will live here at Ashton Place, a strict but kind-hearted governess with three clever pupils who both fear and adore me."

Penelope had read several novels about such governesses in preparation for her interview and found them chock-full of useful information, although she had no intention of developing romantic feelings for the charming, penniless tutor at a neighboring estate. Or—heaven forbid!—for the darkly handsome, brooding, and extravagantly wealthy master of her own household. Lord Fredrick Ashton was newly married in any case, and she had no inkling what his complexion might be.

"Or perhaps I will mumble my way through my interview like a dimwit and be sent home again in shame," she fretted. "Though, alas! There is no home for me to return to!"

At which point the carriage hit a pothole and flew thirteen-and-one-half inches into the air before crashing down again. The driver took this opportunity to break his silence with the brief and heartfelt outburst mentioned earlier, but it is not necessary to reprint his exact words. Fortunately, Penelope was unfamiliar with the expression he used and was, therefore, none the worse for hearing it.

However, she took the interruption as a reminder that wallowing in self-pity, even in the privacy of her own mind, was not the Swanburne way. Instead, she cheered herself with the idea that she might soon have three pupils of her own to teach, to mold, and to imbue with the sterling values she felt so fortunate to have acquired at school. If each child came equipped with a pony, so much the better!

And then, abruptly, they were out of the trees and coming over the crest of a hill, passing between great stone pillars that framed a tall and forbidding black iron gate.

Once through the gate, she could finally see before her the house known as Ashton Place.

THE COACHMAN WAS RIGHT: Ashton Place was a very grand house indeed. It was perfectly situated in the sheltered lowland ahead and big as a palace, with the lovely symmetrical proportions of the ancient Greek architecture Penelope had so often admired in her history books at Swanburne.

From the hilltop vantage of the gate Penelope could see that the surrounding property numbered not in the hundreds, nor the thousands, but in the tens of thousands of acres—in fact, the forest she had just passed through was part of the estate. There were orchards and farms and groups of other, much smaller houses as well. These were the cottages in which the servants lived, and where the blacksmith, tinsmith, and tanner plied their trades. There was even a smokehouse for the curing of fresh bacon, ham, sausage, and all sorts of meat-based delicacies that would nowadays be purchased in a supermarket, uninterestingly wrapped in plastic.

And Penelope noted with delight: There was a barn big enough to house a whole herd of ponies, with their long, lovingly brushed tails and red ribbons braided prettily through their manes—oh, how Penelope wished the job were already hers! But the interview was still ahead, and she resolved to keep her wits about her.

The driveway approaching the main entrance curved around formal gardens of great beauty, now tinged with the first brushstrokes of autumn color. The coachman brought the carriage straight to the front of the house and assisted his passenger brusquely to the ground. A kind-faced, square-built woman of middle age was waiting to greet the new arrival.

"Miss Lumley, I presume?"

Penelope nodded.

"I'm Mrs. Clarke, the head housekeeper. Thank

goodness you've arrived! Lady Constance has been asking for you every quarter hour the whole blessed day. Don't make such a stricken face, dear. You're not late. Lady Constance tends to be impatient, that's all it is. But look at you—you're hardly more than a child yourself! Jasper, see to her bag, please!"

The carpetbag was whisked inside by a young man who appeared from nowhere. As for the trunk of books, which the coachman was struggling to lift—"Leave that in the carriage for now," Mrs. Clarke directed. She jangled the large ring of keys she wore at her waist and gave Penelope an appraising look. "Until we see how things go."

Mrs. Clarke hustled her directly to the drawing room in such a flurry of chatter Penelope barely had time to gape at the grandeur of the house's vast interior. Still, it was impossible to ignore the sheer size and quantity of the rooms, the plushness of the carpets underfoot, the curtains of sumptuous velvet, the way the woodwork shone with the burnished glow of a dark jewel.

The drawing room had been prepared for the interview as if it were a stage set, with two chairs drawn near each other and a tea tray already in place on the sideboard. Mrs. Clarke seemed more nervous than Penelope; she babbled nonstop. "Have a seat there by the window, dear. The air will refresh you. You must be starved! There's tea at hand, but now that you're here I'll bring up a tray of sandwiches in case you feel peckish. Speaking for myself, I can't travel more than a half mile from home without taking some refreshment, and here you've come all the way from who knows where—"

"Heathcote. Excuse me for interrupting," said Penelope, "but what is that unusual sound?"

Mrs. Clark's mouth slammed shut and stayed that way for a count of three, and then flew open again to emit another stream of even more rapid chatter. "What sound? I'm sure I don't hear any sound, certainly not an 'unusual' sound or any other type of sound that one wouldn't normally expect to hear in a busy household such as this—"

"It *is* an unusual sound," said Penelope, tilting her head to listen. "It's coming in the windows. It has a sort of a howling feeling to it."

"A how—a how—!" Mrs. Clarke's rushing river of words suddenly went dry. At that moment a bell rang from some distant place within the house. It was a pleasant, mellow-toned bell, but even the airiest, tinkling

19

chime can be rung insistently and in a panic, and that was unmistakably the type of ringing this was.

Mrs. Clarke gave a small, involuntary yelp. "Ai! That'll be Lady Constance. I'll go tell her you're here and settled. And I'm sure I don't hear anything like a how—a how—well, nothing unusual, to be sure! Here, let me close the windows, dear, so the bugs can't get in—"

At which point, despite the frantic ringing of the bell and Penelope's comment that the breeze was, in fact, quite refreshing and that it would be a pity to shut up windows on such a lovely autumn day, Mrs. Clarke took pains to shutter and bolt every window in the room.

"Would you care for some tea, Miss Lumley?"

"Thank you kindly, I would."

Lady Constance poured the tea herself. "So perhaps she is not *completely* spoiled," thought Penelope with relief. Lady Constance had appeared within moments of Mrs. Clarke's departure, quite breathless, as if she had raced down the halls. Otherwise she was much as Penelope had pictured her: perhaps nineteen or twenty at the most, with blond hair the color of butterscotch pudding and pale, circular blue eyes that were a bit too large for her face.

The round eyes gave her the appearance of a doll, as did her pink-hued cheeks and upturned nose. Penelope knew little about fashion, but even she could see that Lady Constance's tiered silk gown was of the most extravagant style. It called to her mind the words of Agatha Swanburne: "That which can be purchased at a shop is easily left in a taxi; that which you carry inside you is difficult, though not impossible, to misplace."

Lady Constance smiled charmingly. "Well! I have never interviewed a possible governess before! I feel somewhat nervous; you must forgive me."

"It is my first interview as well," Penelope offered, "so perhaps between the two of us we will muddle through."

Lady Constance smiled again and stirred her tea. An awkward moment passed, until the two young ladies spoke at once.

"Where are the—"

"What do you—"

"Pardon me!"

"No, you must go first, of course," Lady Constance declared. Penelope briefly imagined those round, doll eyes were taking in her plain dress and sensible foot-wear, but shooed away the thought as fast as it came.

"I have you at a terrible disadvantage, I realize," Lady Constance went on. "I have seen your résumé and letter of recommendation from Miss Mortimer, so I feel I know a great deal about you. Your headmistress has described you in the most *glowing* terms. But you must have many questions about life here at Ashton Place. Please ask; I will do my best to answer, and we will let the conversation proceed in that way."

She sat back pertly in her chair and folded her hands, as if she were the one in need of a job.

"If you insist." Penelope felt suddenly cautious at the notion of having to interview her prospective employer. "I understand that you are seeking a governess for three children. Perhaps you might tell me their ages and a bit about them."

"Oh!" Lady Constance trilled a strange, forced laugh. "Let us not talk about the children just yet."

Penelope thought this an odd response, frankly.

"Forgive me," she said after a moment. "I don't mean to pry. But a governess for the children is the available position, is it not?" She smiled what she hoped was a warm and friendly smile. "I hope there has not been a mistake?"

"Oh no, heavens, no!" Lady Constance stirred her tea again with vigor, although the sugar had long since dissolved. "We are in dire need of a governess, there is no doubt. It's just that"—she seemed to be struggling to find words and avoided Penelope's gaze—"children are not a very *interesting* topic, I find. That is to say, children are merely—children. All more or less alike. Don't you agree?"

Penelope did not, but she did not say so. It had just occurred to her that Lady Constance was far too young to have school-age offspring of her own. Whose children were they, she wondered, whom Lady Constance found so unworthy of discussion?

"Tell me, then," she said, "about Ashton Place."

Lady Constance brightened at once and launched into an animated description of the house: the history, the architecture, the furnishings. Everything on the premises, she explained, was of the highest quality. The most valuable antiquities had been acquired by her husband's great-grandfather, Admiral Percival Racine Ashton, who had designed and built the house and was himself a figure of historical importance—

"Ahwoooooooooooooooooooo! Ahwooooooooooooooo!"

"Woof! Woof!"

At the sound, the pink circles on Lady Ashton's cheeks visibly shrank and disappeared, as if someone had rubbed them out with an eraser.

"... children are not a very interesting *topic, I find."*

"Pardon me," she said abruptly, rising. She scurried across the drawing room and tugged repeatedly on the bellpull that hung by the door. Penelope could hear it ring in some faraway part of the house.

Mrs. Clarke appeared on the instant.

"I'm terribly sorry, my lady," she said quickly, "we've done our best to keep them quiet—"

"Mrs. Clarke!" Lady Constance interrupted, in a loud voice full of false cheer. "Surely those hunting dogs need to be fed! They sound *entirely* desperate!"

Then she leaned over and whispered rapidly in Mrs. Clarke's ear. Mrs. Clarke clapped her hand over her mouth and listened. When Lady Constance was done, Mrs. Clarke glanced nervously at Penelope and then back to her mistress.

"Of course, my lady, I will see to—the dogs—at once." Then she left.

Lady Constance walked slowly back to her seat, lowered herself carefully, and heaved a most unladylike sigh. Her golden, delicately curved eyebrows frowned in deepest concentration as she glared at the carpet.

Recall that it was Penelope's first job interview; there was nothing for her to compare the experience to except a historical account she had once read describing the interrogation of military prisoners during the

Napoleonic Wars. This hardly seemed relevant. However, the look on Lady Constance's face had grown quite serious, and Penelope guessed that the pleasantries must now be over.

She took a deep breath and braced herself to answer probing questions about her literary and scientific knowledge, her skill at mathematics, penmanship, and musical composition, her grasp of geography and the rules of lawn tennis, and her familiarity with the rudiments of first aid.

"Well," said Lady Constance decisively, after a pause, "Miss Lumley. You are certainly everything I had hoped for in a governess, and more. May I offer you the position?"

"What?" Penelope exclaimed, unable to hide her surprise.

"Forgive me! Of course you need to know the terms. I am utterly hopeless with numbers, but Lord Ashton drew this up for your perusal before he left for business this morning." She handed Penelope a folded sheet of heavy notepaper, monogrammed with a large, decorative *A*.

Penelope opened it and read. The neat writing within indicated salary, number of holidays, sick leave, and so forth. The terms were generous, excessively so.

Ridiculously so, in fact.

"I do hope the salary is adequate! If you require, Lord Ashton will make any necessary adjustments." Lady Constance looked at Penelope with a strangely blank expression on her face and waited for her answer.

"These terms are perfectly acceptable," Penelope finally choked out.

"Excellent, excellent!" Lady Constance sprang from her seat once more and paced around the room. "You must start at once. Today, in fact! I will send instructions to your school—Swansea? Swansong? You must remind me of the name—to send the rest of your things."

"My trunk is in the carriage that brought me from the station," Penelope said. "I have no other possessions." She was suddenly dizzy and thought this must be what people meant when they said that a person was "in shock." But she managed to stand up, and Lady Constance impulsively took her right hand in both of her own.

"Miss Lumley," she said, "may I have your solemn oath that you will embrace the position of governess and fulfill its duties from this day forward? I would hate to endure the *crushing* disappointment I would feel, if you should suddenly change your mind."

Penelope straightened and returned the lady's gaze with as much forthrightness as she could muster, given the rapid turn of events.

"The word of a Swanburne girl is as solemn an oath as anyone could require," she replied. "Have no fear on that account. I accept."

And with that, they both affixed their signatures to the bottom of the letter of terms that Lord Ashton had prepared. Penelope hardly thought this necessary, but Lady Constance assured her that signed, binding contracts were the custom in these parts, a charming formality which she would not dream of omitting.

The Third Chapter

The source of the mysterious
howling is revealed.

WHEN PEOPLE EXPERIENCE a sudden, happy change of fortune, it often comes as a great shock to the system. Reckless personalities may do foolish and extravagant things, such as buying a yacht even if they are prone to seasickness and do not know their port side from their aft, while more cautious souls might busy themselves with trivial, repetitive tasks as they wait for the surprise to wear off. Many a winning lottery ticket holder, upon receiving the news, has spent the entire afternoon methodically sharpening pencils; for all we know some are sharpening still, their winnings yet unclaimed.

Temperamentally speaking, Penelope was more of a pencil sharpener than a yacht buyer. Earlier that very morning, she had been a sleepy girl on a noisy train, but now she was a professional governess in an enormous and unimaginably wealthy house. Part of her was itching to run to the nursery, meet the children, and begin instructing them immediately in Latin verbs and the correct use of globes. She was also eager to write Miss Charlotte Mortimer a letter, telling her the excellent news. But even more powerful than those urges was the urge to unpack her trunk and carpetbag and put her room in order. After all, Ashton Place was her home now, and as Agatha Swanburne often said, "A well-organized stocking drawer is the first step toward a well-organized mind."

Penelope's trunk was brought up to a small, second-floor bedroom, and Mrs. Clarke sent a young lady's maid named Margaret upstairs to help "put away your frocks and bonnets," as the girl explained in her shy, squeaky voice. But when Penelope explained that she had brought many books and few clothes, all of which she would prefer to arrange herself, Margaret curtsied and left the new resident of Ashton Place to her own devices.

With so few possessions, Penelope did not take long to complete her task. Within half an hour her garments were hung up or folded in dresser drawers, and a dozen carefully chosen books were displayed on the small shelf near the door, including her very own brand-new copy of *Edith-Anne Gets a Pony*, a good-bye gift from the girls at Swanburne. It was the first book in the Giddy-Yap, Rainbow! series—an excellent present, of course, but Penelope would have preferred *Silky Mischief,* which was her favorite. No matter; now that she would be earning a salary, Penelope resolved to buy copies of the entire series to read aloud to her pupils—what a happy chore that would be!

The rest of the books she left in the trunk for the present, until they could find their permanent home in the nursery. There would be so much to do! She wondered if she would be allowed to have breakfast with the children and, if so, at what time. The interview with Lady Constance had been so brief and strange that there had been no chance to delve into such details.

"Still," she thought, "there will be plenty of opportunity to learn the ins and outs of my new position 'on the job,' as it were. For now, my sole occupation should be to acquaint myself with my new home—starting with this charming room."

At Swanburne, Penelope had always shared her sleeping quarters. The dormitory halls had each held a dozen girls, two to a cot. So, to have her own bed, in her own room, was an unheard-of luxury. And such a room! The flocked wallpaper had a delicate floral print, the floors were covered with fine Arabian carpeting in a leaf-and-ivy pattern, and the mahogany dresser had drawer-pulls carved in the shape of mushrooms. The four-poster bed was covered with soft, moss-green bedding embroidered with every decorative stitch Penelope had ever learned and many she had never seen before.

Best of all: Tall French windows opened to a small, private balcony. Penelope threw the windows open and stepped outside. How delightful it was! Out here she could sit and take the air, read, admire the gardens near the house, and gaze at the majestic forest in the distance—

"Ahwooooooooooooooooooo!"

"Woof! Woof!"

"Ahwooooooooooooooooooo!"

There it was again—the baying, barking, and howling of the dogs. Could they be hungry again so soon after being fed? Did they miss their master and long for the thrill of the hunt? Or was there something else amiss? The noise seemed to be coming from the direction of the barn.

"Ahwoooooooooooooooooooooo!"

"Woof! Woof!"

"Ahwoooooooooooooooooooooo!"

"There is something beyond hunger in these cries," Penelope thought. She recalled all the times she had tagged along after Dr. Westminster, the Swanburne veterinarian. Once she saw him cure a dog of excessive howling by pulling a single badly rotted tooth. The relief that flooded the poor creature's face when the offending bicuspid was removed had impressed Penelope greatly at the time, and she resolved then and there to never let an animal suffer when comfort could be given.

"Ahwoooooooooooooooooooooo! Ahwoooooooooooooooo!"

Surely some medical difficulty was at work here as well? For this was no ordinary howling, but an anguished cry from the very soul of one—or more— otherwise mute beings!

"Ahwoooooooooooooooo!"

"Ahwoooooooooooooooo!"

"Ahwoooooooooooooooo!"

"Since the children are not yet ready to make my acquaintance," she thought, seizing her cloak, "I have no duties to speak of and, therefore, none I can be accused of shirking."

Her decision was made. She left her room and headed downstairs. She would visit the barn at once, to see what aid she might render to the miserable creature—or creatures—within.

"Miss Lumley! Miss Lumley! Please—wait—you musn't—"

Mrs. Clarke chased Penelope across the grounds, but Penelope had the advantage of youth, not to mention two minutes' head start. The older lady was clearly unused to exercise; by the time she caught up with Penelope, her face looked like the scarlet top of a mercury thermometer just prior to bursting.

"Miss Lumley, it is not proper for you to wander the grounds unescorted—"

"With all respect, Mrs. Clarke, are you deaf?" All Miss Mortimer's advice to Penelope about restraining her natural boldness was forgotten; in Penelope's view, this was a true emergency. "There is a wounded animal in the barn, or perhaps more than one! I am going to see what the trouble is."

"You should wait," Mrs. Clarke gasped, "for Lord Fredrick to return home—"

"By then it may be too late." Penelope quickened her pace even more. "But tell me, how many beasts are in there? And how long have they been carrying on so?"

"Miss Lumley, you don't understand!" The two ladies had reached the barn, and Mrs. Clarke flung herself in front of Penelope, blocking the doors. "It's the children," she said, shaking with upset. "The children are"—*huff, puff*—"inside"—*puff!*—"the barn!"

"The children!" Penelope stopped short. "With those agitated dogs? Surely that is unwise!"

Mrs. Clarke merely stammered, "Eh!—eh!—eh!" but offered no explanation.

Then Penelope had a terrifying thought. "Perhaps the children grew worried for the safety of their beloved ponies and rushed inside to protect them!" she cried. "Surely that is what I would have done, had I been in their place!"

"Ponies?" Mrs. Clarke looked bewildered. "What ponies? We don't have any ponies—"

"Ahwooooooooooooooo!"

"Ahwooooooooooooooo!"

"Ahwooooooooooooooo!"

Without further discussion, Penelope shoved the distraught housekeeper aside, leaned her full weight against the great wooden doors, and pushed them open.

As the sunlight flooded the dark interior, the howling abruptly stopped. Penelope looked around. The barn smelled strongly of leather and hay, but the stalls—at least, those she could see—were empty. The sudden silence was broken only by the panting of Mrs. Clarke, who stood silhouetted in the doorway, clutching her voluminous bosom.

"Hello?" Penelope said, in a soft, soothing tone. "Oh, you unfortunate creatures, are you all right?"

Slowly, noiselessly, something moved inside the barn. Three sets of eyes glinted from the dark corners of the rearmost stalls, where the sun did not reach.

"Come here." Penelope wished she had thought to bring some scraps of meat with her to lure the poor frightened things. "Come out where I can see you."

The creatures obeyed.

They were not dogs, or ponies, or any other kind of four-legged animal. They were three children, and they stared at Penelope with the shining, watchful eyes of wild things.

All three were wrapped in coarse saddle blankets but wore no other clothing, not even shoes. Their hair was long and tangled and of the same distinctive

They were three children, and they stared at Penelope
with the shining, watchful eyes of wild things.

auburn color, which marked them unmistakably as siblings.

They were a boy, whom Penelope guessed to be in the vicinity of ten; another boy, of a size and age approximately three years younger than the first; and a little girl, no more than four or five.

"Well, hello," Penelope said again, even more gently, to hide her astonishment.

One of the children (it was impossible to tell which one) let out a low growl. Mrs. Clarke gasped, but Penelope paid her no mind.

"It is a pleasure to meet you," she said to the children, with all the professionalism she could muster. "I am Miss Lumley, your new governess."

The girl displayed her teeth. The younger boy licked his lips in a most animal-like fashion, while the elder boy merely stared at Penelope. Penelope, who had spent many a useful hour assisting Dr. Westminster at Swanburne, was not in the least bit alarmed. She stiffened her spine and stared back.

He narrowed his eyes.

Penelope narrowed hers as well. Very carefully, so as not to frighten anyone, she made a quiet rumble in the back of her throat that was half purr, half growl.

After a moment, the boy smiled and flopped down

on the hay, rolling over on his back and waving his limbs in the air. The other two watched him carefully; as soon as he was on the ground, they relaxed their tense postures and joined him. Soon the hay was flying everywhere as the children yapped and tumbled over one another quite playfully, until all three lay at Penelope's feet.

Penelope allowed herself a small sigh of relief. "Well, I am glad that's all settled. Now, can you say 'hello'?" She repeated it slowly. "Hello, hello, hello."

"*Hallooooo*," the eldest boy replied, in a soft, lilting howl.

"*Ahwooooo?*" the middle boy added, with a questioning tone.

"*Woof,*" barked the girl, rolling happily on her back. Then she grinned. "*Woof, woof!*"

IT WAS ALTOGETHER IMPOSSIBLE to believe, and yet, standing there in the big wooden barn, with the sunbeams coming in slantwise through the cracks in the shutters to illuminate these three alarmingly unkempt children, Penelope realized there was something strangely familiar about the discovery she had just made. It was poor Silky she was thinking of: His chestnut coat dulled with lack of care, burrs stuck in his forelock, he was distrustful of humans, and prone to bite, at least at first. . . .

"But Silky's behavior was not his fault, for he had known no kindness or tender care in his life. Alas, his new owners, the Krupps, were so cross at having been tricked into buying such a difficult pony for their darling Drusilla that they could not find one grain of sympathy in their hearts for the untrained, unfriendly beast.

"Poor Silky! Soon he would have even more reason to be mistrustful, for in their frustration the Krupps arranged to sell him to Mr. Alpo, the dreaded horse retirer. Mr. Alpo was a shady character who bought unwanted ponies like Silky and promised to 'retire' them to faraway meadows, while all along planning to deliver them to the slaughterhouse—

"No! Edith-Anne couldn't bear to think of it, but what could she do? It was her own Rainbow—dear, sweet Rainbow!—who had the patience to run alongside Silky, hour after hour. Who took the carrots Edith-Anne gave her and nosed them through the fence at her snorting, unhappy friend. Who showed Silky, through patient example, how pleasant it was to be groomed by an adoring little girl, to have one's hooves rubbed with oil, and then to have all those bright red ribbons

braided through one's mane!

"*When Mr. Alpo arrived, halter in hand, to take his prize, how shocked he and the Krupps were to see Drusilla perched happily on Silky's back! His clean coat shone in the sun as he and Rainbow trotted side by side through the course Edith-Anne had prepared for them: circling to the left, circling to the right, a wide figure eight, then diagonals across and back, and a perfect finish in the center. The ponies even took a bow.*"

Penelope had to stop there—partly because the tale was over, partly to wipe her eyes (the story always touched her deeply), but mostly because of the dreadful noise emanating from Mrs. Clarke.

Naturally Mrs. Clarke had been amazed by the sight of three filthy children slowly settling themselves into the dirt and hay at Penelope's feet, drawn by her voice and rapt as kindergartners, although surely they could not understand a word of Penelope's story—but Mrs. Clarke herself was now weeping uncontrollably at the tale of Rainbow and Silky. It took several moments for her to compose herself enough even to blow her nose.

"I think that is all the story we have time for now, children," Penelope said gently. "Now you three must stay here in the barn quietly for a bit, while I go make arrangements for you, but I will come back very soon. And I will bring fresh milk and plum cake when I do."

Whether the children understood her exact meaning was unknown, but the general tone of her words seemed to have gotten across, for there was no more howling. Also, as soon as Penelope rose to leave, the youngest of the three leaped into the warm spot on the ground where Penelope had been sitting and curled up in a ball; the look on her face was very much like contentment.

That started Mrs. Clarke wailing all over again, and Penelope had to lend her a fresh handkerchief before they could make their way back to the house.

THE FOURTH CHAPTER

Lord Fredrick tells a most
unbelievable tale!

PENELOPE'S NOTION THAT THE CHILDREN ought to be
brought inside at once and settled in the nursery met
with some resistance from her walking companion, at
least at first.

"Lady Constance will have to"—*huff, puff*—"give
her permission," said Mrs. Clarke, who, if anyone had
asked her, would have sworn that the journey both to
and from the barn was decidedly uphill.

"Permission? For children to live indoors? I should
think she will!" Penelope exclaimed. "What other

answer could she give?"

To that, Mrs. Clarke gave no reply. The brisk walk back to the house was making her too winded to converse intelligently. "All this trotting to and fro will be the"—*huff!*—"death of me!" she wheezed, although, as you already know, regular aerobic exercise was far more likely to improve her cardiovascular fitness than cause her demise.

Penelope, meanwhile, could not erase the leering, pocked face of Mr. Alpo—for that is how she imagined him to look—from her mind's eye, and it simply made her desire to protect the children all the more urgent. "In that case," she said firmly, "Lady Constance will have to come out to the barn and view the situation for herself."

When they arrived at the house, Mrs. Clarke had to sit down and drink a glass of blackberry cordial to settle her nerves, so young Margaret was instructed to deliver the message to Lady Constance. She soon returned, and even the comically squeaky tone of Margaret's voice could not conceal the sternness of her mistress's reply: Under no circumstances would Lady Constance venture outside that evening. She had retired to her private rooms until further notice and would take supper alone due to a severe headache.

Discouraged but hardly defeated, Penelope felt she had no choice but to plead with Lady Constance in person. Mrs. Clarke looked ready to object, but Penelope laid a hand on her shoulder. "Remember Silky!" she said with feeling, and after that Mrs. Clarke could only nod and wish her Godspeed.

Penelope marched straight to Lady Constance's chambers. Her knock received no answer. She knocked again and called through the door.

"Lady Constance, it is Miss Lumley, the governess! I must have your ear for a moment regarding the children. Their current accommodations are quite unacceptable."

There was a thud and a small crash from inside. After a moment, Lady Constance opened the door a crack and immediately began to wail. "You gave me your word," she cried. "You signed a contract! Oh, please, Miss Lumley! Do not leave us before you begin! I am beside myself. It is only six months since Lord Fredrick and I were married. I am not fond of children in general, and to suddenly become the foster mother to three—and to three such wild, dirty, *incorrigible* creatures—well, I am quite over my head!"

She popped a small chocolate into her mouth, clutched at her temples, and swooned. Luckily

Penelope's reflexes were swift, and she caught her new mistress before she hit the floor.

"Lady Constance," Penelope said, putting her back on her feet, "you must give me leave to settle the children in the nursery. After all, they are in your care." Wisely, Penelope chose not to offer her opinion of the care they had received so far.

"You will need to speak to Lord Ashton about that. I am much too ill to make any decisions," Lady Constance replied, retreating back inside her private parlor. "He will be home within the hour." With that, she slammed her door shut and could not be persuaded to converse any further.

PENELOPE USED THE HOUR WISELY; she made up the children's beds, tidied the nursery, and cleared it of breakable objects. She also instructed the kitchen to bake plum cakes, and the scent of fruit and cinnamon was already wafting through the house. It had even permeated Lord Fredrick's study, where she now sat across from the man himself, waiting for him to speak.

Sadly, the sweet cake-baking smell could not mask the far less delicious odor of Lord Fredrick's cigar. The current master of Ashton Place had the same long and

narrow nose, sloping forehead, and prominent, somewhat pointed ears depicted in the ancestral portraits
that hung on the wall behind where he sat. Penelope
could read the names off the engraved brass plaques
mounted below each painting: *Admiral Percival Racine
Ashton. The Honorable Judge Pax Ashton. Lord Edward
Ashton.* The one of Lord Edward was her least favorite of the paintings (although she could not honestly
say she liked any of them); he was a very rotund man
and even the painted-on buttons of his coat looked as
if they wanted to pop off the canvas. She found his
expression decidedly unpleasant and made a point of
averting her smoke-stung eyes from that harsh, heavy-
lidded gaze.

"Of especially naughty children, it is sometimes
said, 'They must have been raised by wolves,'" Lord
Fredrick finally remarked, tapping his cigar into a
bronze ashtray shaped like a fox. "And, by Jove, these
rascals actually were!"

"I take it," Penelope said, blinking, "that they are
not your own natural-born children, then?"

"Mine? Certainly not. I don't know who in blazes
they belong to, nor do I much care to know." His eyes
glinted with pleasure. "A fascinating trio they are,
though. Suitable for scientific study, what? I suppose

you want to hear the story of where I found 'em."

"It may be useful in explaining their current condition," Penelope said, unflinching. She could forgive the enigmatic coachman, Mrs. Clarke, and even silly Lady Constance for concealing the truth from her until after she had accepted the position, but she really was quite furious that the children had been locked in the barn. Mrs. Clarke assured her that food and water was brought in daily and that they had plenty of hay and the saddle blankets for warmth—but no watercolor paints? No decks of cards? Not a single book to pass the time? Granted the children could not yet read, but surely they could turn pages and admire the illustrations? To Penelope's way of thinking, it approached the barbaric.

"Very well, but I warn you, it's a most unbelievable tale." Lord Fredrick leaned back in his armchair. "Miss Lumley, have you ever gone hunting?"

"No," she said quickly. "I am rather tenderhearted about animals, in fact." She fixed her eyes straight ahead as she spoke. Except for where the paintings hung, the walls of the study were completely covered with stuffed and mounted heads of every imaginable type of beast—from tiny rabbits to a massive, antlered elk. Their sightless glass eyes made Penelope feel intensely observed, and the whole room gave her a sad and queasy sensation in her tummy.

"Tenderhearted, eh? Pity," Lord Fredrick said. "Hunting is a marvelous pastime. Communing with nature and all that! Although it can be dangerous. In my own family there have been some—unfortunate accidents." He jerked his head behind him in the direction of the portraits. "They met gruesome ends, all of 'em. Positively gruesome! All killed while hunting. Except for my father, Edward—although his end was most gruesome of all, in its way. Never even found the body. Anyway, that's how I caught 'em—the children, I mean. It was on a hunting expedition, right here on the grounds of Ashton Place. You can see for yourself; the Ashton Woods are very large indeed. I've hunted in that forest my whole life, and still, there are corners I've never seen."

He paused to chew the end of his cigar. "It was ten days ago. I was out stalking with a pair of my favorite hounds and Old Timothy, the coachman—you've met him, I take it? He's a trusted family servant and knows how to keep quiet in the trees. I often take him out with me, to carry water for the dogs and so forth."

"I have met him," she replied. "He picked me up at the station."

Lord Fredrick nodded and went on with his tale. "We'd ventured deep into the woods, deeper than usual, until we wandered into a clearing and startled some birds into the air. I'd gotten off a shot at a good-sized something or other, maybe a pheasant. Old Timothy was certain I'd hit it, but neither of us saw where it fell, so we set the dogs loose to find it. Instead, they flushed those three ragamuffins out of the underbrush, naked as the day they were born and yapping and howling like a litter of wolf cubs." Lord Fredrick took a deep puff on his cigar. "If Old Timothy hadn't seen what they were in time to stop me, I might have gotten off a shot or two."

"A 'shot or two'—you mean, at the children?" The queasy feeling in Penelope's tummy was growing worse, and she wished she had something safe and familiar to hold: her poetry book, perhaps, or the small pillow cross-stitched with one of Agatha Swanburne's sayings—"Complaining Doesn't Butter the Biscuit"—that her school friend Cecily had made in sewing class and given her for a birthday present two years before.

"I can't see for toffee at distances, I'm afraid," Lord Fredrick confessed, although he did not sound the least bit apologetic. "I can read the newspaper as well as the next man, if I hold it close, but more than twelve paces away and your guess is as good as mine."

"And yet you have managed to . . . " Penelope paused, not knowing a delicate way to say "heartlessly slaughter these many dozens of animals," so instead she waved a hand vaguely around the study at all of the stuffed, staring heads.

"The woods are full of life, Miss Lumley." Lord Fredrick made a swooping gesture with his cigar, leaving trails of smoke in the air. "If you listen for a rustling in the leaves and shoot at it, you're bound to hit something sooner or later. How was I to know there were children living in the forest? On my own estate! It's most irregular."

The smoke made her eyes water and her throat burn, but she was determined not to cough. "And then?"

"Old Timothy always has a rope with him. He's used it in the past to tie up bigger game, like this elk here, and have the dogs drag it home. It was quick work to lasso the children and haul them back to the house. Although I shall not soon forget the racket they made! I was tempted to leave them behind more than once."

Penelope bit her tongue and waited for Lord Fredrick to finish.

"We herded them into the barn. My wife was rather upset, of course, but had the sense to place an advertisement for governess straightaway—and you know the rest. They're filthy and uncivilized, to be sure, but on the plus side you've got a blank canvas to work with." Lord Ashton tapped more ash off his cigar. "I've read your letter of recommendation. Surely a girl of your talents will thrive on the challenge, what?"

"If I am given permission to manage them as I see fit, I have no doubt that their better natures will prevail," Penelope answered rather boldly. "However, at this very moment, they are still locked in the barn wearing nothing but blankets, and Lady Constance has not yet given me leave to move them into the nursery."

"'As you see fit,' what is meant by that? Ah, you are concerned about my wife's feelings, is that it? Now, Miss—Lumley, is it?—I realize that Constance is rather high-strung about all this, but I assure you, as soon as they can say 'please' and 'thank you' and perform some simple tricks, her maternal nature will blossom like a rose. She'll feel calmer about it in the morning. For tonight, let things stay as they are. There'll be less trouble that way all around."

"But sir," Penelope pressed, "children should sleep in beds, in clean pajamas, and have bedtime books read aloud—"

"After years of living in the wild, one more night in

a barn won't kill 'em." Lord Fredrick pushed his chair back in a way that made it clear: The conversation was finished—Penelope's side of it, anyway. "You can read stories to 'em in the nursery tomorrow, assuming they don't have fleas, of course. Remember, Miss Lumley, they were found on my property and that means I can do with 'em as I please. Finders keepers, what? Here, look: I have chosen names for all three." He took a small note card out of his vest pocket and handed it to Penelope. "See that they learn to answer to these. It is very tedious to say 'Hey, boy!' or 'Hey, girl!' and get no reaction. Even my hounds can come when called."

"As you wish." Penelope took the card from him without bothering to look at it, since her eyes were suddenly blurry with tears, and this time not from the smoke. "It shall be our very first lesson."

By the time Penelope had made her way back to the barn carrying a basket full of fresh-baked plum cakes and a large pitcher of milk, the sun had already dipped far below the horizon. With no daylight to illuminate its interior the barn was quite dim, and yet with so much dry hay scattered everywhere, Penelope was afraid to light a candle. The children seemed perfectly comfortable in the dark, though, and at the smell of the cakes, they gathered close to their new governess without a trace of fear.

Penelope had brought three tin cups from the kitchen and poured each full of milk to wash down the cakes. The children lapped at the milk like puppies and sniffed at the cakes for a long time before deciding to eat them. Penelope demonstrated what to do, and soon their faces were covered with cake crumbs and milk mustaches. If not for the wild, squirrels' nests of hair, lack of clothes, and overall unwashed condition, they would have looked practically childlike.

Penelope hated to let them eat with such grubby hands, but "First things first," she said aloud. "Tonight we must make friends and grow used to one another. Tomorrow we can think about giving baths."

The children looked at her quizzically, tipping their heads from side to side in a way that reminded Penelope of a cocker spaniel she had once seen staring at itself in a mirror. Then she remembered the card from Lord Ashton, still unread in her apron pocket.

"The three of you are now the wards of Lord Fredrick Ashton, and in his capacity as master of the household, he has chosen names for you." She slipped the card out and read. "You," she said, looking at the eldest boy, "are to be called Alexander. Can you say it?

Alexander," she pronounced again, clearly.

"Alawoooooo," he repeated.

"Very good!" She glanced at the card. "It says here, you are named after 'Alexander the Great, the legendary commander who mercilessly conquered the Persian Empire and was said to drink too much wine.' Hmm. That is an odd choice."

"Alawooooo!" he said again, with feeling.

"As for you," she said, turning to the smaller boy, "you are to be called Beowulf. 'Beowulf was a fearless warrior of old, who slew monsters and dragons until he met a bloody and violent end.' A most unsavory namesake, in my opinion, but that is what Lord Ashton has written here. Can you say Beowulf?"

"Beowoooooo," the boy said proudly.

"Excellent," Penelope praised. "And now for our littlest pupil. Heavens! It appears that Lord Ashton has named you—well, let me read it. 'Cassiopeia, after the vain and arrogant queen of the ancient Greeks who tried to sacrifice her own daughter to the sea gods.' How dreadful! But it will have to do." She was about to ask the little girl to repeat her name, but the clever child had been watching the other two and beat Penelope to the task.

"Cassawoof!" she yelped. "Woof! Woof!"

"That is good enough for now." Penelope sighed. The names were very ill-chosen in her opinion. For one thing, Cassiopeia was quite impossible to spell.

"Tomorrow we will begin our lessons, children," she said, putting away the card. "And take baths. But now we must go to sleep. Good night, Alexander. Pleasant dreams, Beowulf. Sleep well, Cassiopeia."

Then, since Penelope knew the best way to teach anybody anything was by setting a good example, she lay down in the hay and closed her eyes. Immediately, the children piled up against her like a litter of puppies and did the same. In that way, the four of them stayed quite cozy, the whole night long.

The Fifth Chapter

A difficulty with trousers
is soon resolved.

As you probably know from personal experience, there are children who love to take baths, and there are children who absolutely do not. It took some trial and error, but Penelope soon discovered that Alexander would get in the tub only if the water was quite cool and perfectly still. Cassiopeia preferred hot water but was frightened of the soap. Once in, Beowulf could hardly be pried out of the bath; he would have soaked all day if permitted.

"This is not a Russian spa, where we can lay about

and take the waters all day long," Penelope said to him, cheerfully but firmly. "We have lessons to do, and—the dress goes on frontward, Cassiopeia, arms through the holes, but please dry off first—and the sooner we get started, the better!" Soon Beowulf was out of the tub and wrapped in a thick towel, like the others.

It was a new day, and Penelope had taken Lord Fredrick's words to heart—as far as she was concerned the previous night would be the last one these three children would spend anywhere but in a bright, tidy nursery, with plenty of toy soldiers, a miniature china tea set, and a copy of *A Child's History of England* near at hand.

Penelope had smiled ear to ear to find a supply of child-sized clothing, washed and pressed, in a basket by the barn door at sunrise, with a note that read: "For the three 'Silkies,' from your friend, Mrs. C." But she was quite determined that the children must follow her to the house and wash up before they could dream of putting on clean clothes. By means of much gentle cooing and calling of "Here, children! Follow Miss Lumley! Keep your blankets around you, come, come!" she had been able to accomplish the journey from barn to bathtub without difficulty, except for a good deal of barking and scuffling along the way and one small incident when Alexander chased a squirrel halfway up a tree and had to be lured back down with treats.

"That Mrs. Clarke," Penelope thought with gratitude, as she tugged the dress over Cassiopeia's freshly shampooed head. "Although excitable and in need of calisthenics, she is also warmhearted and efficient. She would have had the makings of a Swanburne girl, given the right training and encouragement. Well, it is never too late to improve oneself!"

Meanwhile, the noise made by the plumbing and the sight of the water gurgling down the drain was a source of fascination to the boys. "It drains clockwise, as it always does in the northern hemisphere. That is known as the Coriolis effect," Penelope noted. The children stared at her blankly, and she sighed. "But we will continue our studies of the earth's rotation at another time. Now, gentlemen, it is time to put on your clothes."

She spoke with some trepidation, due to the fact that Penelope had lived most of her life in an all-girls' school and had as little knowledge of how to fasten boys' trousers as Alexander and Beowulf. The bathroom, as was the style in very wealthy houses of those days, was a large room with a separate screened dressing area.

Hoping for the best, Penelope handed their clothes to the two boys and indicated that they should go behind the screen and put them on as best they could.

Of course, she reasoned as she waited, if they needed a male instructor in this urgent matter of the trousers, Mrs. Clarke could send up that young Jasper fellow who had carried her trunk upstairs so capably. "Perhaps I ought to call for him now," she thought. "This does seem to be taking a long time."

She took a step nearer to the screen and inquired, "Alexander? Beowulf? Are you almost dressed?"

"Alawooooo" came from behind the screen.

"Beowooooo" followed immediately after.

"Cassawoof!" Cassiopeia barked obligingly from the loveseat on the other side of the room. She had one woolen stocking pulled halfway up her arm and was flapping it around with delight.

"That is a marvelous display of your skill at introducing yourselves, children," Penelope said, "yet I am curious to know how the pants are coming along. Show me the pants, boys, if you please!"

Alexander and Beowulf stepped out from behind the screen, grinning foolishly and pushing each other in front. Beowulf had put his arms through the pant legs and had a shirt tied loosely around his waist.

Alexander and Beowulf stepped out
from behind the screen . . .

Alexander's pants were on his legs, but inverted, with his feet stuck through the bottom ends of the trousers and the waistband encircling his ankles.

Cassiopeia burst into fits of laughter while Penelope, eyes modestly shielded with one hand, walked across the room to give the bellpull a tug. "What a good beginning that is, boys!" she said encouragingly. "Now I am going to ask Mrs. Clarke to summon our friend Jasper. He can show you some of the refinements of gentlemen's dress, in case we should ever want to go out in public—oh, Mrs. Clarke! You are very quick."

"I was just bringing up fresh towels and heard the bell." She leaned close to Penelope and whispered in her ear. "How did you ever get them to follow you inside the house? A week ago they had to be dragged into the barn with a rope!"

"A week ago they were being hunted with a rifle and were frightened out of their wits," Penelope replied hotly. "They are no different from any other strays—I mean, children. They will follow anyone who feeds them and is kind. Many thanks for the clothes," she added. "The 'Silkies' have been washed and curry-combed, and I think you will find their appearances much improved."

Mrs. Clarke stuck her head in the bathroom to see

this remarkable sight. Instead, she got an eyeful of the inventive and somewhat revealing outfits fashioned by the boys.

"Pardon me!" she shrieked, clapping her hand over her eyes. Her sudden outburst caused the children to whimper in fear and hide behind the bathtub.

"Now, now," Penelope said soothingly. "Mrs. Clarke, I was just going to ask you to send that boy Jasper up, so he could demonstrate to these young gentlemen the correct technique for getting their trousers on."

"I'll have him come in at once," Mrs. Clarke said, fanning herself. "Dear me! Shall I have tea brought up? They look—thirsty."

The children had now calmed themselves and were lapping water out of the faucet with their tongues.

Penelope considered the housekeeper's request. "For the time being, the children and I will take our meals in the nursery. And, Mrs. Clarke, if you could put the children's milk in small saucers instead of cups, it would be most appreciated."

THE NURSERY WAS A SUITE of sunny rooms on the third floor of the house, where the children would be "safely out of the way," as Mrs. Clarke put it. There was a night nursery, where the children would sleep (under normal circumstances, a boy of Alexander's age would have been old enough to have his own room, but the children seemed inseparable, and given their unusual background, Penelope thought it unwise to try to pry them apart). The adjoining day nursery was where they would eat, play, and do their lessons.

The children seemed to take their new home in stride. They had nothing to compare it to, and in any case their attention was fully taken up with the novelty of being clothed. Beowulf and Cassiopeia marched behind Alexander in a comical parade, crossing back and forth in front of the dressing mirror and then darting around the back in an attempt catch the elusive, wild-haired children who seemed to live behind it.

But the bright, spacious nursery, with its well-stocked classroom and large chest of never-used toys, struck Penelope as almost too splendid, and she wondered if she would ever grow accustomed to it. Of course she had always felt fortunate to attend a school where the girls were treated kindly and fairly and provided with a well-rounded education, rather than just the usual domestic subjects (although, really, everyone ought to know how to stitch on a button, and that will be true as long as there are buttons to pop off). The fact that Swanburne girls dressed plainly, ate simply, and were unspoiled by luxuries merely made the true riches of Penelope's upbringing all the more evident to her.

It would have been pleasant to have parents, of course, or at least parents whom she could more clearly recall. Penelope had been scarcely four years old when she was delivered to Swanburne's doorstep, for reasons that had never been made clear. She recalled being told about a mother and father who needed to take a long, dangerous journey and would someday return for her—or perhaps that was something she had read in a book. It was hard to be sure after so many years, and she had no one to ask. But there was always Miss Mortimer, who was like a mother to the girls; all in all, Penelope felt her lot in life had been rather lucky. Seeing these three waifs in their cast-off state broke her heart a little. She was glad that their days in the forest were now over, and there was now a chance to make up for what had been lost.

"If I can provide them with a fraction of the steady care that Swanburne and Miss Mortimer have given me, then all will be well," she thought, before blurting: "Dear me, Cassiopeia, mind your dress! I realize it may be faster to go on all fours, but I think you will find your stockings will last longer at the knee if you walk upright. Here, allow me to demonstrate."

The teachers at Swanburne were firm believers in the prompt writing of thank-you notes, and despite all the excitement of her new responsibilities, Penelope was determined to get a letter of appreciation in the post to Miss Charlotte Mortimer that very day. After all, if not for Miss Mortimer's finding the advertisement, being so firm and encouraging about Penelope's application for the job, and then writing such a heartfelt letter of recommendation—why, Miss Penelope Lumley would not be a governess at all! She began the letter by thanking her former headmistress profusely, and then went on:

As for my three pupils: They are Alexander, Beowulf, and ~~Cassiopea~~ ~~Cassiopia~~ Cassiopeia (Forgive the inkblots! The name is new to me and will require practice). Because of their canine habits and tendency to howl, it is believed that they were raised by wolves. This is to my advantage in some respects, since I have always got on famously with dogs. I shall write Dr. Westminster separately to thank him; his animal training techniques have so far proven invaluable.

After addressing the basics of personal hygiene this morning, we attempted our first real lesson, which comprised going 'round the nursery and naming common objects (in English for now; I must put off French and Latin for a short while, until the children are more used to life indoors). They do not seem to speak any language other than barking, howling, and some strange guttural noises they use among themselves. But they are clever mimics, and I have no doubt that they will soon be prattling away.

Despite their sad history of neglect, they are alert and healthy looking—thin but strong-limbed, with shining auburn hair that is even more vivid in color now that it has been washed and the burrs have been taken out.

I hope all is well at Swanburne. I miss its halls, and all the girls, and, most of all, you, but have so far been much too busy—and too surprised!—to feel sad.

With affection and deepest thanks,

Your own,

Penny

Penelope had just finished signing her name to the letter and was about to start on one to Dr. Westminster when the nursery door creaked open.

"Miss Lumley? May I enter?"

Penelope stood up. The children followed her example, although Cassiopeia first sat on her haunches and had to be nudged to her feet by Alexander.

"Good morning, Lady Constance!" Penelope smoothed her dress and hoped Lady Constance had not seen the children biting one another, as it might have given the wrong impression. "We were not expecting visitors so soon, but you are most welcome to come in, of course."

"Is it safe?" Lady Constance whispered hoarsely, hovering in the doorway. "Mrs. Clarke has been telling everyone that the children were naked as monkeys."

"Indeed they were, but only while getting out of the bathtub. There was some brief difficulty with the trousers, but with the help of your manservant Jasper, it was resolved." Penelope glanced at the boys. "So far the pants have stayed up, so I think the lesson was well learned."

With that assurance, Lady Constance took one hesitant step inside the nursery and allowed herself a look at its occupants. The children were clean, and although their clothes were a bit large and their hair was long and loose, they looked far more like children than wild animals.

Penelope stood straight and still and fixed the children with a strong look. "Allow me to present Alexander, Beowulf, and Cassiopeia. Children, this is your mistress, Lady Ashton."

"Hello, children," Lady Constance said in a shaky voice.

"Hewwooooooo!" the three children intoned.

"Oh my heavens!" Lady Constance covered her ears. "What a din!"

The children, who had spent the morning repeating the words that Penelope had tried to teach them, likewise covered their ears and howled, *"Whatawooooo! Whatawoooo!"*

Lady Constance looked mortified. "They are not making fun, my lady," Penelope quickly explained. "Until they can read well enough for textbooks, I must teach through the use of example and imitation. May I demonstrate?"

"If you must," said Lady Constance weakly. She seemed eager to leave, but Penelope had already turned to the children.

"Let us play fetch again, as we did earlier," she said to them, "and show Lady Constance what you have learned. Alexander! Ball!"

Alexander loped across the nursery, fetched a ball out of the toy trunk, and brought it back to drop at Penelope's feet. She patted his head. Beaming, he took his place again with the others.

"Beowulf! Soldier!" Beowulf scampered to the toy

box and returned with a tin soldier.

"Now, Cassiopeia—doily!" With some guidance (on the first attempt she grabbed a doll in a lacy dress), Cassiopeia succeeded in bringing a doily back to Penelope.

"You see," Penelope said to Lady Constance with pride, "in this way they have learned the words for many common items, such as ball, doily, and so forth. And they have also learned to stand in line. That is a skill that comes in useful in any classroom."

"How fascinating," Lady Constance said, not sounding interested at all. "Miss Lumley, will the boys be having haircuts soon? Their appearance is positively poetic!"

The boys' hair was quite long, hitting the middle of their backs, but it was clean and brushed and Penelope saw nothing objectionable about it for the time being. "They will, when they can sit calmly in a barber's chair," she said. "I think it would be unsafe to rush too soon into any activity where razors are involved."

"I suppose." Lady Constance pursed her lips in distaste. "But if they are to continue living in the house, ust be presentable. What if important friends of shton's drop by?"

hich point, Cassiopeia scampered over to Lady

Constance's feet, seized one of her hands, and licked it, from top to bottom. Then she gazed up at her, looking very pleased with herself.

"She means to show that she likes you," Penelope started to explain, but Lady Constance was already recoiling toward the door.

"Ugh! Ugh! Now I must go wash at once! Who knows what *diseases* these creatures must carry, after living so long in the wild?"

"There is a basin and washcloth right here, my lady, allow me—"

"No!" Lady Constance shrieked, before gaining control of herself. "That is to say, no thank you, Miss Lumley. Please continue with your lessons." She backed out of the nursery, cradling her hand as if it had been burned. "Clearly, you have a *great* deal of work ahead of you."

LADY CONSTANCE, ALTHOUGH WRONG about some things, was certainly right when she observed that Penelope and the children had a great deal of work ahead of them. And yet it occurred to Penelope that the children should not be kept indoors too much at first; it might prove a shock to their systems and cause them to catch cold. On the other hand, if she let the children outside, she wondered if they might run off into the forest, or roll in the dirt and ruin their clothes, or (perish the idea!) attempt to catch and eat any of the pigeons that wandered the grounds near the house. That would be repulsive, as well as ruin the children's dinner.

But: "The best way to find out how fast a horse can run is to smack it on the rump," as Agatha Swanburne once said, and so, at midafternoon, after arming herself with pocketfuls of biscuits, Penelope took the children out. If Mrs. Clarke or Lady Constance questioned what they were doing out of the nursery during school hours, "nature studies" would be her reply. Obviously the children were already well acquainted with nature, but giving plants their botanical names would serve as a good introduction to Latin, as well as to each kingdom, phylum, class, order, family, genus, species, and so forth.

However, Penelope was already feeling quite worn out from her first full day as a governess, and privately she hoped the children would forego educational pursuits and simply romp about in the falling leaves and wear themselves out a bit before supper.

As it turned out, she need not have worried about the children running away. If you have ever secretly begun to feed a stray litter of kittens by putting an open can of tuna on the back porch at night when no one was looking, you know quite well that the problem is not that the animals run off. It is that they refuse to leave you alone ever again. Penelope never had to use the biscuit treats, and although the children were quite noisy and full of playful barks and growls, the worst thing that happened was that Beowulf put one knee right through the fabric of his new trousers.

"Pants can be mended, never you fear," she consoled, when he showed her the damage.

"Pantsawooooo?" he said, with a puzzled expression on his face. Then, much to Penelope's amazement, he called his siblings over. "Alawooooo! Cassawoof!" They came at once and obediently looked at his knee.

"Pantsawooooo!" he explained.

"Pantsawooooo," they agreed sadly.

Penelope could hardly contain her excitement at this remarkable exchange, but when she looked up to see if there was anyone nearby to share it with, she spotted only the bent form of Old Timothy, the coachman. He was watching them from a distance, half hidden in the shadow of one of the old chestnut trees that grew near the house. He might have been lurking there for some time, but for how long?

She nodded once in his direction, to make sure he knew she had seen him. He nodded back. Then he slipped away.

Being watched made Penelope uneasy, although she could not fully explain why. "I suppose I am unused to what it means to live in such a large house, with so many people going about their business in every direction," she thought. "Perhaps he is curious to see how the children are faring. After all, he was the first to spot them in the forest. It is possible that he will take a grandfatherly sort of interest in them."

Of course, Penelope had no personal experience of what a grandfatherly interest might be like, since she had no grandparents of her own, at least that she knew of. On the rare occasions that she had asked about her somewhat mysterious past, Miss Charlotte Mortimer had always encouraged her to concentrate on her studies and not trouble herself about questions that simply couldn't be answered—at least not yet.

Penelope nearly always found it best to follow Miss Mortimer's advice. Although, watching the children scamper about, Penelope could not help feeling curious about to whom they might really belong and what sort of person might have been so cruel—or so desperate—to have left them in the woods of Ashton Place.

Then she remembered Lord Fredrick's words about the old coachman, as well as the coachman's own remarks. "He can be 'quiet in the trees,' indeed," she thought. "And recall that silliness about 'It's lucky a house can't speak'—I would wager it is Old Timothy, not the house, who could tell the Ashton family secrets, if he so chose!"

Even with so many interesting thoughts in her head, Penelope found herself stifling a yawn. She was tired and hungry and imagined the children were as well. "It is time to go in, children," she said, gathering the trio around her. "It is time for suppawoooo—I mean, for supper."

Accompanied by the children's happy howls of "Suppawooooo! Suppawoooo!" the weary governess shepherded her three pupils back toward the house that was now home to all of them.

THE SIXTH CHAPTER

*The children are given a
name that sticks.*

AND SO, UNLIKELY AS IT ALL SEEMS, that is how Miss
Penelope Lumley's career as a governess began.

The challenges posed by her new pupils put her in
mind of one of the more well-known sayings of Agatha
Swanburne. In fact, it was the saying Swanburne Academy had taken as its motto, chiseled into the stone arch
over the entryway to the main building in which classes
were held. Penelope had gazed upon the inscription
countless times since she was a young girl no bigger
than Cassiopeia, but its message had never seemed so

apropos to her personal predicament as it did now: "No hopeless case is truly without hope."

Truly, sometimes Penelope felt as if the wise founder of her alma mater were speaking directly through the ages, just to her.

Penelope's days soon fell into a rhythm: She would wake in her charming room and suffer a pang of homesickness, which she would soothe by reading from her poetry book or adding a few lines to her latest letter-in-progress to Miss Mortimer. Then she would go to the nursery, where she would rouse and dress the children, take breakfast with them, and settle in for the day's lessons.

To her credit, Penelope's enthusiasm for providing the children with a top-notch education remained in full force. She still hoped to begin French and Latin as soon as practical. She yearned to read her favorite poems aloud to them, to demonstrate basic techniques of watercolor painting, and to explain the difference between the Baroque sensibility and Romanticism in classical music, although she sometimes got them mixed up herself. However, other lessons proved more urgent and, surprisingly, more complicated.

For example, Penelope had never before realized how difficult it was to explain the logic behind such common household paradoxes as: Standing on the floor is perfectly correct; standing upon the loveseat is not. Going up the stairs is often necessary, but climbing up the side of a bookcase never is, even if one has accidentally let loose of a yo-yo while trying to learn to go 'round-the-world, and one was merely trying to get a better look at where it may have landed. Or so Alexander attempted to explain, in his halting, howling way.

Convincing the children of the importance of these distinctions required careful demonstration, a great deal of repetition, and the occasional use of tasty treats, yet Penelope remained patient and kind. "After all," she thought, "the children can hardly be blamed for their uncivilized condition—no more than poor Silky could be blamed for his, or the Poor Bright Females of Swanburne Academy for their lack of solvent relatives!"

She thought of her pupils as unusual, not unteachable. In fact, she found them endearingly eager to please (however, she did learn not to leave her shoes lying about unattended, as Beowulf had a tendency to gnaw). But clever as she was, even Penelope was often unable to predict what would set them off.

Squirrels, for example. Squirrels proved to be a virtually irresistible source of provocation. At the mere glimpse of one of the nibbling, button-eyed, bushy-tailed creatures, the children would freeze to attention, stare, hunker down, and approach silently in low, even crouches until within striking distance. Then they would pounce. It was riveting to watch—nowadays it would make a fine documentary for broadcast on a nature channel on cable television—but there was a seemingly endless number of squirrels on the grounds of the estate, and they rendered Penelope's outdoor excursions with the children much too full of excitement to be truly enjoyable.

Nor did staying indoors provide an escape. Every day, the little gray-furred beasts would scurry tormentingly through the branches that hung outside the nursery windows, which threw all Penelope's attempts to teach odd and even numbers into chaos. And there was always the worry that the children might actually catch one of the dimwitted rodents. Given Penelope's tender feelings about animals, she did not think she could bear to see her pupils tear one limb from limb without becoming extremely upset.

After giving the matter a great deal of thought, Penelope came upon what she felt was an ingenious solution.

"I shall devise a squirrel desensitization program,"

she thought. "Through careful repeated exposure, I will teach the children not to give two figs about squirrels. I wonder if it has ever been done before?"

It had not. In fact (and unbeknownst to her, of course), Penelope had just made an important breakthrough in the field of behavioral psychology, one that would not be repeated by medical professionals for many decades yet to come. No doubt that is why none of the books Penelope had brought with her from Swanburne contained the information she sought. Nor did she think Dr. Westminster had ever undertaken such a project. Further research would be required, and that meant a trip to the library was in order.

She made sure the children were safely occupied with chewable objects, obtained the necessary permissions from Mrs. Clarke, and paid her first formal visit to Lord Ashton's library—an enormous, musty-smelling room she had peeked in longingly every time she walked past it.

It was chilly and dark, even on a sunny afternoon, with many more books than even the library at Swanburne had contained. The section on animal behavior was exceptionally well stocked. In short, Penelope was in library heaven, and she prepared to start taking notes. She quickly found a book on wolves, which provided many thought-provoking tidbits of information and even shed light on some of the children's more intriguing habits—the way Alexander, for instance, would occasionally discipline his siblings by knocking them to the ground and rolling them onto their backs. Or the way Beowulf would rise from his bed during the night and gaze out the nursery window, mournfully *ahwoo*ing for hours on end. Or Cassiopeia's tendency to scamper closely after Penelope and sit at her feet the instant she stopped moving.

"But was it truly necessary to select such *extraordinary* names?" It was Lady Constance's voice, and she sounded both cross and quite nearby. "They will only serve to draw attention."

Lady Constance and Lord Fredrick had entered the library; Penelope could glimpse them through the stacks. A perplexing development! She had asked permission to enter the library so she could not be accused of trespassing, yet the encounter felt impossibly awkward, especially since the couple seemed to be in mid-argument. She did not know what to do except freeze in place and wait for an opportunity to make her presence known.

"Personally I would have christened them Tom, Dick, and Fanny," Lady Constance nattered on. "However did you settle upon Alexander, Beowulf, and Cassiopeia?"

Lord Ashton chuckled. "Simple! I started with A and proceeded down the alphabet in sequence."

"You are ridiculous," she said, perhaps fondly or perhaps not; it was difficult to tell.

"I was merely being prudent," Lord Fredrick replied, in his merry, thoughtless way, "in case we find another twenty-three grubby children wandering in the forest. Twenty-six letters in the alphabet, what!"

Even without being able to see her face, Penelope had a feeling that Lady Constance was not amused by this remark.

"And what about a surname?" the lady pressed. "Surely you don't mean to call them by the name of Ashton?"

"Why? What's wrong with the name Ashton?" Now Lord Fredrick was the one who sounded cross. Penelope realized the moment had passed when she might have revealed herself without embarrassment. Now she had no choice but to remain silent and unseen and wait for the ordeal to be over.

"Nothing is wrong with the name of Ashton, dear husband! That is the point. Ashton is an ancient and noble name. A name ripe with glorious history. A name with illustrious and, dare I say, wealthy associations.

What will happen when *we* have a child, Fredrick? *That* is who should bear the family name. Not these—these—incorrigibles!"

A strange, faraway look clouded Lord Fredrick's face. "Children of our own, quite right, quite right! Bound to happen sooner or later; I had forgotten about that."

Lady Constance giggled shrilly. "Forgotten? Oh, Fredrick, you are *utterly* ridiculous sometimes; that must be why I married you. But honestly, clawing and scratching and baying at the moon—can you imagine such a creature as heir to the estate?"

"Of course not." He sounded suddenly severe. "These three vagabonds are not Ashtons. Not Ashtons at all. They are the Incorrigibles, indeed—and that is what we shall call them, from now on."

He wandered perilously close to where Penelope was hidden, but merely to pull a book off the shelf. After he turned away, Penelope shut her eyes in the childish hope that it might render her invisible. Now all she could do was listen:

"Ah, here's what I'm looking for! *The Huntsman's Almanac.* I keep this copy shelved in my study. The maid must have put it away."

"Surely you are not planning another hunting

"They are the Incorrigibles, indeed—"

expedition! And in this chilly weather! I do believe you see more of your men friends from the club than you see of me, Fredrick."

"What a worrying mind you have, Constance. My expeditions are none of your concern. As for the almanac, I merely wish to check the weather predictions. The farmers will want to know what sort of winter to prepare for—"

The couple left, still conversing. Penelope held her breath until their voices had completely faded. Only then did she dare open her eyes. She was alone in the library once more.

"Alexander Incorrigible!" she thought, appalled. "Beowulf Incorrigible! Cassiopeia Incorrigible! Three more unwieldy names would be difficult to imagine. But, as the saying goes, 'Nothing good was ever learned from eavesdropping, so mind your business and let others mind theirs.'"

She was right, of course, and not just because Agatha Swanburne had said so. Eavesdropping rarely leads to the desired result. One hides under the bed hoping to discover whether or not a surprise party is being planned for one's birthday, and instead learns that indeed there was, but the festivities have been canceled due to one's cousins all coming down with pinkeye simultaneously. The danger and dust bunnies are hardly worth the trouble.

Penelope knew this, but in her defense it should be noted that she had not planned to eavesdrop in the first place. The experience had been thrust upon her with no warning, as if she were a character in a comedic French play. Overall, she felt she had handled it well.

"Still, let this serve as a reminder," she thought, as she made her way back to the nursery, her now-full notebook tucked under her arm. "I will have the children read *Hamlet* as soon as it is practical. There are some useful cautions against eavesdropping to be gleaned from that. In the meantime, we shall deal with the squirrels."

PENELOPE'S RESEARCH WAS COMPREHENSIVE, and her plan of action was theoretically sound. Yet her squirrel desensitization program did not instantly meet with success.

She made adorable squirrel dolls for the children in hopes of teaching them to think of squirrels as beloved pets, but they joyously gnawed the dolls to pieces. The white cotton stuffing was tossed everywhere, making it seem as though a blizzard had hit.

She hung drawings of squirrels all over the nursery, expecting that the constant exposure would soon cause the children to grow bored with the idea of squirrels altogether. Alas, the pictures simply made the children so agitated that no quiet work could be done. However, Penelope did become very adept at drawing squirrels.

Finally, she decided that more direct measures were called for. This difficulty, like most others, would be solved only if faced head on. Penelope instructed the children to bundle up in coats and scarves. Then she took them outdoors, bid them sit at the base of a tree, and laid it on the line. "You must develop self-control, that is all there is to it," she said firmly, looking at each of them in turn. "No more chasing squirrels."

Alexander started to growl, but Penelope would have none of it. "Mind your manners, Alexander! As Agatha Swanburne once said: 'If it were easy to resist, it would not be called chocolate cake.' Now look up, all of you—and *don't move.*"

They looked up. The branches were mostly bare of leaves now, and the squirrels were in full-fledged autumnal hysteria, frantically seeking nuts and burying them everywhere their tiny one-track minds could think of.

The three Incorrigibles stared, hypnotized by the

sight. The squirrels raced deliciously from branch to branch. They scurried tantalizingly up and down the trunk, heedless of any danger—so close, yet just out of reach—

"Easy, children," Penelope soothed. "That's it, just stay as you are, you can do it—"

Beowulf was the first to crack. He was on the second branch before Penelope could catch him, and she got hold of only his ankle, but it was a firm grip. Cassiopeia, too small to make it up the trunk, ran in rapid circles around the base of the tree, yapping excitedly, while Alexander crouched on the ground and gazed upward with darting eyes, ready for action should Beowulf succeed in flushing the squirrel in his direction.

"Down, Beowulf!" Penelope pulled hard on his ankle and brandished some tasty biscuits with her free hand. "Down, down, down! Everyone, as you were!" She maneuvered all three of them back into position at the base of the tree and implored them to stay, just for a few seconds this time. Then there were biscuits for all.

Exhausted, Penelope hustled the children back to the nursery and made them copy alphabets on slates with their slate pencils, while she drank three cups of milky tea to settle her nerves.

The whole exercise was repeated daily for a week, and each time Penelope made the children sit still under the tree a bit longer before rewarding them. The children would quiver and tremble (Beowulf would sometimes drool), but they were soon able to resist actually chasing the squirrels, for whole minutes at a time. Even so, Penelope knew this was a lesson that would need frequent brushups.

Now and then she would spot Old Timothy watching them, but he never spoke to her, nor to the children. If she caught his eye, he would offer a silent nod. Then off he would slink.

THE SEVENTH CHAPTER

*The pow'r of poetry leads to
an unwanted invitation.*

"LUMAWOO?"

This is what the children had taken to calling Penelope. She trusted that "Miss Lumley" would come soon enough, but when they said "Lumawoo," it was perfectly clear to whom they were speaking, and she knew no disrespect was intended. In fact, she rather liked the name. It reminded her of the nicknames babies give to favorite objects, their ba-bas and blankies and noo-noos and so forth.

"Yes, Beowulf?"

"Poem!"

The breakfast dishes had only just been cleared away. With Alexander's assistance, Penelope had succeeded in heaving another log onto the hearth, and the nursery was feeling decidedly cozy. Beowulf's request further increased Penelope's sense of contentment. "Do you want to hear a poem, Beowulf? You are in luck; I was planning to read more poetry today. After lunch, I thought we might have a go at 'The Wreck of the Hesperus.'"

Beowulf shook his head. "No Wreckawoo."

Penelope frowned. She was the teacher, after all, and the decision ought to be hers. However, she had already made a false start with Dante's *Inferno* and had to abandon reading it partway through, and she did not want to repeat this misstep with the Hesperus. She had chosen Dante because she found the rhyme scheme pleasingly jaunty, but she realized too late that the *Inferno*'s tale of sinners being cruelly punished in the afterlife was much too bloody and disturbing to be suitable for young minds. Penelope could tell this by the way the children hung on her every word and demanded "More, more!" each time she reached the end of a canto and tried to stop.

"Now, now, don't be stubborn, Beowulf. 'The Wreck

of the Hesperus' is by a poet called Longfellow, and it is a very dramatic tale. I think you will like it. It even has a shipwreck in it! Although, I suppose that's obvious from the title."

Beowulf just stood before her, shaking his head no.

"That is not what you meant?"

"No Wreckawoo," he repeated. "Wulfie am *talk* poem. Lissawoo!" By which he meant, "Listen!" Then he stood still and recited, with real feeling:

"Moon, moon, moon.
Night, no moon? Dark.
Night, yes moon? Light!
Yes, moon!
Ahwooooo!"

The other two children clapped enthusiastically. Penelope was astonished. "Beowulf, did you write that poem yourself?"

He smiled sheepishly and nodded.

"I am—well! I am most impressed!" Penelope had begun reading poetry to the children in the belief that it would improve their English faster than lists of spelling words ever could. Besides, she personally found poetry very interesting, and since her students were more or less blank slates when it came to literature, she felt she might as well do what she liked. (As you may already know, the Latin term for "blank slate" is *tabula rasa*, a phrase the Incorrigibles would no doubt be exposed to a little further on in their educations.)

But Penelope had not yet dared suggest the children begin composing works of their own. Clearly, she had underestimated them.

"Me!" Alexander jumped up. "Lumawoo, me, me!" He grinned and eagerly hopped back and forth.

Penelope was so surprised, she had to sit down on the toy trunk. "You have a poem also, Alexander? Well, this is one delightful surprise after another, children! Let's hear it, then. Beowulf, come here next to me, and let your brother have the stage."

Obediently Beowulf sat down, and Alexander stepped up to declaim:

> *"Yum, yum. Squirrel!*
> *No! No!*
> *Yum, yum. Cake?*
> *Yes! Yes!"*

He bowed deeply, which is something Penelope had taught the boys to do as part of their training in good manners. Cassiopeia leaped up from her customary spot at Penelope's feet and curtsied, just to stay in the spirit of things. Then she too turned to her governess, her eyes sparkling with excitement.

"Cassawoof!" she declared. "Cassawoof, too!"

Penelope could hardly believe it. "My heavens! You don't have a poem, too, do you, Cassiopeia? If you do, I think I shall have to lie down for the rest of the day to get over the shock."

In answer the little girl shoved her slate forward.

"Don't tell me you wrote it down—ah, what is this? There is a curved shape, rather like a crescent, and another just like it. Well, that is very good, also." Penelope smiled indulgently. "And what do you call your drawing?"

"Moon plus moon, two moons," Cassiopeia explained modestly.

Penelope clapped her hands in delight. "What a dazzling display this has been, children! Your enthusiasm for learning is what every teacher dreams of awakening in her pupils. I must say I am pleased."

The three young scholars stood before her, wriggling with pride. Penelope longed to give each one a hug, but she knew that a wise governess always maintains a certain professional reserve. She quickly settled on a different reward.

"Allow me to repay you for your wonderful work by sharing a poem—no, not the 'Hesperus,' we will save that for later. But it is one of my personal favorites. Perhaps you will find it as compelling as I do. It has haunted me for as long as I can remember."

At fifteen, Penelope was much too old for a ba-ba or a noo-noo, but the truth was her poetry book served a similar, comforting purpose, and she often kept it close at hand. Now she slipped it out of her apron pocket and opened to a well-worn page. "The poem is called *'Wanderlust.'*"

"Wanderlust?" Alexander seemed to like the sound of the word and said it again. *"Wanderlust!"*

"Yes." Penelope felt suddenly shy. "It means 'having a strong desire to travel.' The poem was originally written in German but I have it only in translation. It begins like this:

"I wander through the meadows green,
Made happy by the verdant scene—"

There was a tap at the nursery door. Penelope marked her place with a ribbon and went to answer. It was Mrs. Clarke, and right away her eyes flew to the book in Penelope's hand.

"Good morning, Miss Lumley! Reading to the children, I see. Is it one of those delightful pony stories, by any chance?"

"Not today, Mrs. Clarke. In fact, it is a rather melancholy German poem, which we are reading in translation. But you are welcome to stay nevertheless."

Mrs. Clarke looked disappointed. "Poetry? It disagrees with me, I'm afraid. All that *bum-de-bum-de-bum-de-bum*; it's like riding in the back of a hay wagon on a bumpy road. Gives me a sick feeling in the tummy. But when you crack open the covers of dear Rainbow again—well, I wouldn't mind listening in for a page or two." The soft expression on her face quickly gave way to her usual brisk efficiency. "Sorry to interrupt, Miss Lumley, but Lady Constance has asked to speak to you. She wants a full report on the children's progress."

Penelope clutched her poetry book tightly. "Now?"

"Now, yes. She is in her private parlor."

Penelope turned to the children. "Very well. We will finish *'Wanderlust'* another time. Behave yourselves and practice adding your moons until I return from my conversation with Lady Constance."

She gulped and suddenly felt quite nervous,

although she would have been hard put to say why. Cassiopeia hugged her tightly around the legs. *"Wanderlust,* Lumawoo!" Alexander said warmly, while Beowulf nodded in agreement, and this bolstered her courage a great deal.

ALTHOUGH THEY HAD SPOKEN briefly on a number of occasions, Penelope had not been summoned to a private audience with her mistress since the day of her job interview. This time, no tea was served. Nor did Lady Constance ask her to sit, although she herself was perched in a delicate chair before her vanity table, while Margaret, the squeaky-voiced lady's maid, braided and pinned her hair into an elaborate updo.

"Miss Lumley, thank you for coming to see me. Forgive me for being at my *toilette,* so to speak. I have a luncheon engagement and am running tragically late! And Margaret is so slow, I am quite out of sorts."

"Not at all. I am glad to be here," Penelope said, although privately she thought she might prefer to be lashed to the mast of the real *Hesperus* as it sank into the howling sea than have to stand there awaiting Lady Constance's questions. It was like one of those distressing dreams in which one must take a quiz for which one has had no chance to prepare.

"So, Miss Lumley, have the Incorrigibles been civilized yet?" Lady Constance gave her a wan smile. "Are they still baying at the moon? I hear reports from the kitchen that those pupils of yours are consuming an alarming amount of ketchup. Perhaps you can explain."

"They are unaccustomed to eating cooked meats," Penelope answered, trying not to sound defensive. "The ketchup is a temporary solution."

In fact, Penelope had discovered that the children would eat meat only if it was served extra rare and completely covered with ketchup, but she did not see the need to go into all that with Lady Constance. And truthfully, this "Incorrigibles" business got under her skin! She may have officially been a governess for only a few weeks, but it wounded her professional pride to have her students talked about in such a cavalier manner.

"How revolting," said Lady Constance primly, followed by, "Ouch! Careful, Margaret! You are pulling my hair too tightly."

"Sorry, ma'am!" the girl squeaked.

As she watched poor Margaret turn pale and loosen the braid, Penelope was overcome by a particular type of irritated feeling that is known as "having one's feathers ruffled." Her urge to push Margaret aside and give Lady Constance's butter-colored hair a hearty yank was difficult to squelch.

"I understand you wish to hear a progress report on the children's education," she said on impulse. "I am pleased to say that they are surpassing all expectations. Three more studious and dedicated pupils would be difficult to imagine."

"Really." Lady Constance could not turn her head because of the braiding, but she glanced sideways in Penelope's direction. "I find that hard to believe."

"Only this morning, each of the boys recited a poem of his own authorship. And Cassiopeia shows signs of mathematical genius."

"Astonishing. This is a very glowing report," Lady Constance said, sounding dubious. In fact, it was rather too much aglow, but Penelope was in for a penny, in for a pound, as they say. "And what of other subjects? French? History? Geography?"

Because of the time spent on the squirrel desensitization program, Penelope had not yet made much headway in either French or history, but she recalled a particularly energetic game of fetch-the-ball the children had played using one of the globes earlier in the week. She had scolded them for it at the time, but now she chose to take a different perspective on the incident.

"Geography is actually one of the subjects the children enjoy most. Christiania!" The word burst from her lips nearly of its own accord.

"Pardon me?" This time Lady Constance whipped her head around to look at Penelope, which caused Margaret, still holding tight to the end of the braid, to get thrown sideways, like the last car of a roller coaster going around a sharp curve.

"Christiania is the capital of Norway," Penelope explained, red-faced. "It just came back to me."

(For those of you with maps close at hand, you will note that the city of Christiania has long since been renamed Oslo. This is a perfect example of why so many children prefer to play catch with their globes rather than study geography with them, for place names and the boundaries of nations have a tendency to change the very minute one is done memorizing. By the time you read this, it is quite possible that the name of your own hometown may have been changed from something charming such as, say, Sweet Maple Ridge to something more sleek and modern, like Aluminumville. This is called progress, and there is no stopping it, so it must be cheerfully borne.)

"Hmm," Lady Constance said, sounding thoughtful. "Well, well! I must say, I am surprised to hear they are progressing so rapidly. This news changes my plans topsy-turvy."

"Plans?" At once, Penelope wondered if her well-intended exaggerations might have been unwise.

"Yes. A month from now I intend to host a holiday ball here at Ashton Place. To be frank, I had planned to send you and the children away for the duration, but for some reason my husband particularly requested that the Incorrigibles attend. That is why I sent for you today, Miss Lumley! I expected you would tell me the children were in no way prepared for such an event, and that would be the end of it. But writing poetry? Mathematical genius? Now you have taken away all my excuses."

"A party?" Penelope repeated, stunned. "With guests?"

"Naturally with guests! It would not be much of a party otherwise." Margaret had finished; Lady Constance's hair was now an alarmingly complex knot of yellow braids. She dismissed the girl with a wave, and Margaret seemed only too happy to go, although she cast a sympathetic look toward Penelope as she backed out the door and hurried away.

Lady Constance turned and faced Penelope. "Well, I am disappointed, but at least my husband will be pleased. Lord Fredrick was not keen on the idea of the party at first, but when he seized upon this notion of the Incorrigibles attending, he changed his mind. Isn't it strange? Why he insists on keeping them here at Ashton Place I do not know. There are certainly enough orphanages in England to take them in. But 'finders keepers' he says, and laughs! Oh, how ridiculous men can be. You are lucky, Miss Lumley. A girl of your station will likely stay a spinster and not have to concern yourself with such matters."

"'I wander through the meadows green,'" Penelope thought to calm herself, "'made happy by the verdant scene—'"

"But I told Lord Fredrick in no uncertain terms: I will not permit the *peculiarities* of these three untamed waifs to disrupt my party plans. After all, it will be my first Christmas as lady of the house! I would be devastated, *utterly* devastated, if anything were to spoil the occasion."

Now, there is a scientific principle that states: Once a train has left the station and is going along at a good clip, it is often fiendishly difficult to slam on the brakes, even if you are clearly headed for trouble (the same holds true for horses that have already left their barns). This principle is Newton's very first law of motion and was considered old news even in Miss Penelope Lumley's day.

Penelope had taken physics at Swanburne and, thus, knew all about Newton's laws of motion. Still, she felt that a final, desperate, and heroic attempt to change the course of events that now led inexorably and disastrously to the children attending Lady Constance's party seemed called for, and so she gave it her all.

"Lady Constance, your plans for a holiday ball sound delightful, and I am sure the children would hate to miss it," she began, "but coincidentally, I was intending to ask you if I may take them on a ski holiday in France until after the New Year. It would be a suitable reward for all their hard work, and we would be out of your way for the ball."

To give you an idea how final, desperate, and heroic this suggestion was, it should be noted that Penelope had never skied in her life, nor had she ever been to France that she could recall, nor did she know precisely where one might ski in France. However, she assumed that any country with so sterling a reputation must be equipped with mountains somewhere; the rest of the necessary information she knew she could easily find in an encyclopedia.

"Send the children away at Christmas? What would people think of me?" Lady Constance's sarcastic laugh was so piercing, Penelope wanted to cover her ears. "No, now I am quite decided, and in any case Lord Fredrick will not have it any other way. The Incorrigibles will attend the ball. Based on your glowing report of their progress, I have every confidence that you will have these poets of yours ready in time."

"Writing poetry is one thing," Penelope said cautiously, "but a party? Parties tend to be large and loud and full of strangers. I am not sure—"

"*Tsk-tsk!* What could be more natural than children enjoying themselves at a party? And you have more than a month to prepare. Read your history, Miss Lumley; military invasions have been planned in less time than that! They will need new clothes, of course. I will ask Mrs. Clarke to arrange a visit from the tailor and dressmaker. Impeccable table manners will be required, that goes without saying." She drummed her pink nails on the top of the vanity in concentration. "Let me see, what else? There will be entertainment, charades, and so forth; it would be most desirable for the children to participate."

At the mention of charades, Penelope felt a glimmer

of hope. Charades at least might go over well, as long as the tableaux did not involve any reference to small, bushy-tailed animals that stored nuts in their cheeks.

Lady Constance stood and attempted to control her great round skirt, which bobbed around her comically. "Whoops! These new cage crinolines take some getting used to," she said gaily. "But they are all the fashion. Very well, I must be off to my luncheon engagement. As for the Incorrigibles and the ball: Mark my words, their future rank in society will depend on the impression they make that evening."

"Of course, Lady Constance," Penelope replied dully. "May I be excused now? The children are waiting in the nursery, and it seems we have much to accomplish before the holidays."

Lady Constance nodded, and Penelope turned to go. She made it as far as the door before Lady Constance called out.

"One more thing, Miss Lumley! Make sure the children know the schottische!"

"Yes, my lady." Penelope could barely hide her gloom. "The schottische it shall be."

THE EIGHTH CHAPTER

*A homesick governess
asks: What would Agatha
Swanburne do?*

PENELOPE RETREATED TO THE NURSERY, accompanied only by the sharp reproach of her own miserable thoughts.

Disaster! The holiday ball would be a disaster, and it was all Penelope's fault. If only she had not been so proud and stubborn! Why had she felt the need to exaggerate the children's progress just because Lady Constance's remarks had annoyed her?

The truth is that one cannot go through life without

being annoyed by other people, and this was just as true in Miss Penelope Lumley's day as it is in our own. Annoyance is a fact of life; one ought not to lose one's grip because of it, and in doing so Penelope realized she had made a grave and potentially catastrophic error.

December! For the first time in her life Penelope found herself wishing December would slow to a crawl. Why must Christmas come so soon? She bleakly wondered if there was any chance the children could be made ready for such an important and complicated public appearance in such a short time. It seemed doubtful, but she would have to try. She rued the hours that would be lost from their studies; now all her efforts would have to focus on preparations for the party.

Orphanages! Why, oh why had Lady Constance brought up the subject of orphanages? The word itself was enough to send a chill through the bones of many a Swanburne girl, for quite a few of those Poor Bright Females were actual orphans, and no matter how plucky and well cared for an orphan may be there is still something regrettable about having become one; that fact cannot be soft-pedaled. Nearly as tragic was the fact that many of the non-orphan girls might just as well have been, since they were stuck with the kind of distant, unfeeling relatives who never visited or remembered birthdays, graduations, or any other occasion when a card or small gift would have been deeply appreciated.

Penelope's circumstances fell somewhere between orphan and non-orphan. She had parents somewhere, she was nearly certain, and she did not choose to think they were unfeeling. She simply did not know who they were or when she could expect some sign of their return. Miss Mortimer had always advised her to assume that things had happened for best and focus on her studies, and Penelope had done so willingly. But still, that awful word—*orphanages*—it was enough to give one an itchy rash just thinking about it.

"Yet Lord Fredrick did say 'finders keepers,'" Penelope reminded herself. No doubt it was nothing more than a glib remark, meant as a joke, but it sounded as if Lord Fredrick had no intention of sending the children away. Probably this orphanage business was just careless talk on Lady Constance's part. But if the children failed to make a good impression at the party, might that change?

And, as if all that were not upsetting enough: What on earth was the schottische?

The words circled in Penelope's brain like vultures: *Disaster . . . December . . . orphanages . . . the schottische!*

Disaster . . . December . . . orphanages . . . the schottische!
To the beat of this ominous refrain, she trudged up
the stairs to the nursery, one heavy footfall following another, like a condemned prisoner climbing the
gallows.

The children were blissfully unaware of the festive
fate that lay in store for them, and were delighted at
their governess's return. She did not have the heart
to tell them the bad news about the holiday ball right
away—new party clothes, honestly! Could anything
be more dreadful?—but she was too upset to resume
teaching or even to read melancholy German poems
in translation.

Distracted and glum, she had the children repeat
the fetch game, but instead of retrieving objects from
the toy trunk (a task which had become laughably easy
for them by now), Penelope sent them to the bookshelf
to find books on topics that she called out at random.

"Gibbon's history!" she ordered. Grunting, Cassiopeia lugged back the first volume of *The History of the
Decline and Fall of the Roman Empire.*

"Rhetoric!" Beowulf found a collection of the
speeches of Cicero and offered them proudly.

"Astronomy!" Alexander returned with a dusty volume about solar eclipses.

"Perspective drawing . . . algebraic equations . . . music theory . . ." Now giggling at the impossibility of keeping up, the children fetched books at random and stacked the volumes at their governess's feet. Yet this tottering shrine to the breadth of human knowledge served only to mock Penelope cruelly, for she knew full well that among the large and varied collection of works she had brought in her trunk from Swanburne Academy, there was not a single book that explained how to walk, talk, dress, speak, or eat at a fancy grown-up party. And, at present, that seemed to be the only knowledge that mattered.

ONCE MORE PENELOPE VISITED the library, this time in hopes that she might plumb the mysteries of the schottische, but to no avail. It was neither a breed of dog nor a type of undergarment (these were her first two guesses). Nor was it a weapon, a style of cooking, or something to keep one's head dry in foul weather. In the end, it was Mrs. Clarke who solved it.

"'Shah-teesh?'" Mrs. Clarke repeated, puzzled, when Penelope desperately confided her dilemma. "It sounds edible to me. Maybe you spread it on crackers for a light meal?"

"I don't think so. I have already done a thorough

survey of appetizers, and it was not among them." Penelope felt defeated. "It's something Lady Constance wants the children to know about for the party. I am quite at a loss, and I dare not ask her."

"For the party? Ah-ha! You must mean the Scottish!" Mrs. Clarke clapped her hands in delight. "It's a kind of dance, Miss Lumley. I'm surprised you don't know it! Did they not teach you any dancing at school? The Highland Scottish, we used to call it, but I suppose that's not fancy enough for a society ball. It's a bit like a polka with a reel thrown in. Here, I'll show you."

As it turned out, the schottische was a very energetic type of dance. Mrs. Clarke's attempt to demonstrate lasted no more than a minute before she had to sit down and take out a handkerchief to mop her forehead.

"I used to dance like that all night long when I was younger," she declared. Her face was red, but her eyes were a-twinkle. "Margaret will have to teach you; she's a spry young thing. I haven't the wind for it anymore." Mrs. Clarke jangled her ever-present ring of keys in a thoughtful manner. "So, Lady Constance wants you to learn the schottische, eh? I've heard about the new craze among the high-society types. Folk dancing, they call it. A bit of country-bumpkin fun to break up those long, tiring days being rich. Makes you wonder what

111

the gentry'll do for entertainment next! Wash dishes? Beat the rugs? The housemaids could use the help, surely!" With that, Mrs. Clarke made herself laugh so heartily, her face turned scarlet all over again.

Penelope got a strange thrill hearing Mrs. Clarke speak so freely of the "high-society types." It allowed her to feel as if she had been accepted as part of the household, which was pleasant—but it also made her realize that her place in the household was among the servants. That was something new to consider, for, unlike Margaret and Mrs. Clarke, Penelope had a first-class education, probably better than Lady Constance's (if one excluded dancing, fashion trends, and hair care as topics of study, of course).

"Hmph," Penelope thought to herself. "There is something not quite right about that. I will have to give it further analysis when time permits." For the moment, however, the schottische must have her full attention.

Margaret was first surprised and then delighted at the notion of giving a dancing lesson to the children. She appeared in the nursery at the appointed time, having changed out of her maid's apron and into a clean frock, accompanied by the young servant Jasper. For some reason, Jasper's presence made Penelope

112

feel even more bashful and awkward about this whole dancing business than she already did, but once Margaret explained that the Highland Scottish was properly done as a partner dance, Penelope had to admit that Jasper's participation would come in useful.

The boys were delighted to see their trouser instructor again. They proudly showed him how securely their buttons were fastened and how nice and straight their pant legs hung. Margaret fussed admiringly over Cassiopeia's long auburn hair (the boys' "poetic" tresses had finally been trimmed by one of the farmers who was known to have a knack for sheep shearing, with no injuries reported).

Despite her personal misgivings, Penelope thanked both of the young servants profusely for their willingness to spend their time furthering the children's education.

"Oh no, it's my pleasure, miss! Dancing is more fun than changing the beds," noted Margaret.

"Or slaughtering the pigs for bacon," Jasper agreed. "Less messy, too. What do you say, Meg? Shall we show 'em how it's done?"

First, the two of them demonstrated. The children watched, rapt, but Penelope's attitude remained skeptical. If knowing the exact steps of complicated and exhausting dances was so important, why had this subject not been taught at Swanburne? Penelope had no objection to dancing on principle, of course. She had read about the Imperial Russian Ballet in Saint Petersburg, where the world's greatest dancers went to study and perform. The gravity-defying performances of those dancers, with their impossible leaps and lifts, and ballerinas who spun 'round tirelessly, like those on the tops of music boxes—well, *that* sounded well worth the trouble. A few lessons in that sort of dancing and a pretty costume to match would have been a perfectly pleasant way to spend the afternoon.

But Penelope's reverie about the Imperial Russian Ballet was soon drowned out by the ruckus of two ruddy-cheeked servants careening dangerously around the nursery, while the children stamped their feet to keep time. She forced herself to watch: As far as she could tell, this schottische business was nothing more than a pair of people holding hands and skipping, followed by a fast twirl and some hops, and then more of the same. The fact that the partners were expected to maintain contact throughout these clumsy contortions seemed a certain recipe for sprained ankles and embarrassing collisions.

And yet Jasper and Margaret were beaming as they

hopped and skipped—almost as if they were enjoying themselves! The children eagerly copied the steps, and what they lacked in accuracy they made up for in verve. Like the children of Hamelin falling in line behind the Pied Piper, the three merry Incorrigibles stomped and jumped and spun.

"Wait till you do it with a fiddler playing—that's the real fun of it!" Jasper laughed. "Now you, Miss Lumley! You must learn it, too." He held out a hand to Penelope. Margaret, whose cheeks were now flushed a pretty shade of pink, threw him a smile and moved back, out of the way.

As Penelope reluctantly stepped up to take Jasper's hand, she could not help noticing how his eyes lingered on Margaret in a way that was nothing short of, well, lingering. Margaret returned his gaze, shy and bold at the same time. It was all quite peculiar; Penelope did not know what to make of it.

"Here we go!" Jasper cried, stomping one foot to set the tempo. He took Penelope's left hand in his right, circled his other arm around her waist, and off they went.

"Step-step-step, *hop*, step-step-step, *hop*—and skip, and skip, and skip, and skip!"

Margaret sang a pretty, wordless melody in her high

voice; her natural squeakiness sounded conveniently like the scratch of a fiddle. The children clapped their hands and danced along behind. After a few halting circumnavigations of the nursery, Penelope felt she had started to get the hang of it. It was not wholly unpleasant, and Jasper was doing the bulk of the work.

"Now for a reel!" he cried, and before anyone could protest, he led the parade out of the nursery. Soon they were dancing down the halls.

"Wait!" Penelope was breathless as he spun her into a fast twirl, but she was laughing, too. "We will disturb Lady Constance!"

"Lady Constance is out shopping, and Lord Fredrick is at his club, Mrs. Clarke said so," Margaret reassured her. "Mind the lamps, Jasper! Oh, this is very merry, very merry indeed!"

And next the revelers were schottisching down a flight of stairs (where they were met with the pressed-lip smiles of housemaids); they reached the end of a hall, a turn was made, a door accidentally pushed open—

There was the stale smell of cigar smoke. A whiff of formaldehyde. And the unmistakable funk of dead fur.

The eyes of the ancestral portraits glared, unmoving from their canvases, yet always following, like the moon.

"It is Lord Fredrick's study!" Penelope clutched her heart. "Children, don't look—"

It was too late. Alexander, Beowulf, and Cassiopeia were aghast. Their eyes swept the walls like searchlights, revealing each mounted, stuffed head in turn: the furred ears, the massive pronged antlers, the bared teeth—all the dead yet sickeningly lifelike trophies of Lord Fredrick's hunting habit.

There came a low growl from Alexander, who had locked eyes with a bear. Beowulf snarled fiercely at the sight of a stuffed squirrel on a bookshelf, but did not pounce. The smell of death was too strong.

Then Cassiopeia sucked in a great raw breath and let it out again in sobs. Her tiny outstretched hand pointed across the room, where the proud, gray head of a wolf stared balefully from yellow glass eyes.

"*Maaaaaaaaaaaa!*" she wailed. "*Mahwooooooooo!*"

"Come away, come away." As quickly as she could, Penelope shepherded the children out the door. She tried to sound in control, but there was a catch in her voice. "Back to the nursery, everyone. This is no place for us."

Their eyes swept the walls like searchlights . . .

THE NINTH CHAPTER

*A missing book causes
quite a ruckus.*

IF YOU HAVE EVER OPENED a can of worms, boxed yourself into a corner, ended up in hot water, or found yourself in a pretty pickle, you already know that life is rarely (if ever) just a bowl of cherries. It is far more likely to be a bowl of problems, worries, and difficulties. This is normal and should not be seen as cause for alarm.

Yet it is also true that the very same troubles that loom catastrophically large one day can seem like small potatoes the next, particularly if even worse troubles have popped up to take their place. An example:

Penelope's frantic worry about learning the schottische had now been wholly replaced by her concern for how the children would cope with their accidental visit to Lord Fredrick's study.

Truly, it had been a tragic encounter with taxidermy. Penelope would not soon forget the horrified looks upon those three innocent faces. She hoped the shock would not undo any of the progress the children had made in their lessons, and tried to offer soothing distractions.

"Let us turn our thoughts to wild adventure on the high seas," she suggested, after an unusually glum breakfast in the nursery. It was the morning after the incident. The children had picked at their food and not even ketchup could tempt them to eat. Penelope felt self-conscious gobbling away while the children were so gloomy, but the strenuous dancing of the previous day had given her a hearty appetite that no amount of stuffed dead animal heads could erase. Secretly she tucked some buttered rolls in her pockets for later.

"At long last, today we shall be fascinated and entertained by 'The Wreck of the Hesperus,'" she continued, once the dishes were cleared away and the trio of sad children had gathered obediently around her. "It is by Henry Wadsworth Longfellow. That is the poet's name. Can you say it? Longfellow."

"Longfell*ooooooo*," they repeated listlessly.

What a miserable sight they were! Penelope wondered if she ought to ask what was wrong, but as she already knew the answer, she decided it would be best to press on with the poem. Reading aloud was a task she enjoyed; it allowed her to pretend she was a famous actress on the London stage, which she thought might be an interesting career if only it were not so scandalous. Also, the working hours for famous actresses ran late into the evening, and Penelope had always preferred early bedtimes.

She sat up straight in her little chair and cleared her throat. "Longfellow, correct. Well done, children. Before I begin, you ought to know that a schooner is a type of ship. The rest should be self-explanatory. Here we go:

"It was the schooner Hesperus,
That sailed the wintry sea;
And the skipper had taken his little daughter,
To bear him company.

"Blue were her eyes as the fairy-flax,
Her cheeks like the dawn of day,
And her bosom white as the hawthorn buds,
That ope in the month of May.

"'Ope,'" she paused to explain, "means 'open.' It is an example of what is called poetical language. Do you have any questions?"

The children were still and silent—too silent, in Penelope's opinion. She looked at them for a moment through narrowed eyes and turned back to Longfellow.

> "The skipper he stood beside the helm,
>   His pipe was in his mouth,
>   And he watched how the veering flaw did blow
>   The smoke now West, now South.

> "Then up and spake an old Sailòr,
>   Had sailed to the Spanish Main,
>   'I pray thee, put into yonder port,
>   For I fear a hurricane.

> "'Last night, the moon had a golden ring,
>   And to-night no moon we see!'
>   The skipper, he blew a whiff from his pipe,
>   And a scornful laugh laughed he."

Penelope was about to demonstrate what she thought Longfellow might have meant by a "scornful laugh." But at the mere mention of the moon, the children had gone pale.

"Ahwooo!" Alexander crooned a soft, agonized howl.

"Ahwooooo!" Beowulf joined him, still soft but urgent.

"Ahwoooooooooo!" Cassiopeia threw her head back and gave it her all. *"Ahwoooooooooo! Ahwoooooooooo!"*

The howling was dreadful and went on for quite some time. Penelope put the poem down with a sigh; they would return to the Hesperus later. Now, she felt she must intervene. She waited until it seemed the noise had reached its peak and was on the way down.

"Children, listen. Listen to your governess, please!" With a few final *ahwoo*s and barks, the din subsided. Penelope tried to assume the same firm, gentle tone Miss Mortimer had always used to good effect on the girls at Swanburne.

"Now, I am well aware that being raised by wolves can be considered an undesirable start in life," she began. "But truly, which of us do not have obstacles to overcome? Whining—or howling or what you please—is not the solution to any of life's problems. I realize that there have been challenges. I assure you there will be more."

Alexander's teeth were half bared. Beowulf was gnawing on his own shoe, and Cassiopeia let out a tiny whimper, but Penelope felt she had their attention. She continued, "Abandoned in the forest as infants, suckled by ferocious smelly animals, forced to wear uncomfortable party outfits, and made to learn to dance the schottische—this is simply the way life goes. Hands must be washed before dinner nevertheless. *Please* and *thank you* must be said, and playthings must be put away when you are done with them. Are we agreed?"

They sniffed and nodded. Cassiopeia had no handkerchief and dabbed at her eyes with the hem of her skirt, but Penelope did not feel this was a time to scold.

"Very well. Today you three are too excitable for poetry, so let us tidy the nursery and work on our multiplication tables. The weather is poor, so we will skip our walk and spend the time sketching."

It was lightly raining, but the real reason for staying indoors is that Penelope did not want to risk dealing with the squirrels or the mysteries of the forest or any other unexpected jolt to the nervous system until such time as the children were thoroughly recovered.

When, or if, that time might come—well, that remained to be seen.

"BLAST IT ALL!" The sound of Lord Ashton's voice boomed through the house, up the stairs, and into Penelope's room at the far end of the corridor, all the way from the first floor drawing room. "Blast it, I say! Has anyone been in my study?"

At least, that is what he may have said. Penelope couldn't quite make it out; it was rather late at night, her door was closed, and she was already in her nightgown, tucked under the covers (the fire in her bedroom had long since gone out, and the air was quite chilly).

Penelope was not yet sleeping, however. She was lost in her own thoughts: thoughts about the children and the moonlight coming in her window, and about how the mystery of not knowing what one's future held paled next to the mystery of not knowing all that one's past already contained. Despite her calming words to the children, in the privacy of her own heart Penelope was still haunted by Cassiopeia's plaintive cry at the sight of the wolf's head in Lord Fredrick's study. Yes, the Incorrigibles had been cared for by wolves in the forest; that much was clear from their frequently canine behavior—but they were children, not wolves. Somewhere in the world there was a human mother who had given birth to these three; a human father who had, perhaps, taught young Alexander how to catch a ball, or watched, smiling, as toddler Beowulf played peekaboo with newborn Cassiopeia.

But then, what had happened? Had these parents,

like her own, also had a sudden need to flee? If so, why leave the children in a forest? Why not find a proper home for them or send them to a reputable school like Swanburne? Penelope longed to talk the whole business over with Miss Mortimer; it was too late now to get up and write a letter, but she resolved to set pen to paper as soon as practical.

Downstairs, there was a muffled and decidedly female reply to Lord Fredrick's outburst, a brief consoling murmur that seemed to aggravate him all the more—

"But it's *not* where I left it, which means someone must have taken it! Blast, blast, blast! Now *who's* been in my study?"

Then there was quiet, broken only by heavy, deliberate footfalls that trudged their way dutifully around the house, accompanied by the jangling of keys. They slowed noticeably when on the stairs (where they were further punctuated by wheezing), and then resumed their previous tempo and grew louder, until they sounded quite close—

"Miss Lumley?" It was Mrs. Clarke, right outside the bedroom door. "Sorry to disturb you. Are you awake?"

Penelope sat up in bed and pulled the covers close around her. The thrill of an unexpected late-night visit was just the thing to knock all those melancholy musings out of her head; it held the promise of adventure. She wondered if there had been a fire, or an outbreak of a contagious disease, or if a band of ruthless highwaymen had been spotted nearby!

"Yes, come in," she called.

The door opened with a creak. The light from Mrs. Clarke's candle entered a step before the woman herself; she wore her dressing gown and a frilly white nightcap. Through chattering teeth she explained, "I apologize for the hour, Miss Lumley. I was in bed myself, as you can see. But Lord Fredrick returned very late from his club, and now he can't find his blasted—sorry, his almanac." She heaved a weighty sigh. "He has ordered me to inquire 'this instant' if anyone has seen it or set foot in his study while he was away. Why in blue blazes a misplaced book couldn't wait until morning I don't pretend to understand! But now I've done as my master asked, and I bid you good night."

Her duty fulfilled, Mrs. Clarke turned to go.

"The children and I did set foot in his study," Penelope blurted, "but I assure you that is all we did."

Mrs. Clarke stopped; she fixed Penelope with a stern and cautionary look. "Miss Lumley, do you see this nightcap covering both my ears? I assure you, I can't hear a blessed thing when I have it on."

"I said, the children and I *did* set foot in the study—"

Mrs. Clarke yawned loudly. "Whatever it was that you said, I am certain it was nothing worth repeating, and at this hour you should be asleep in any case. Now I will go—"

Alas, Penelope did not pick up on Mrs. Clarke's meaning and kept talking despite the older lady's shushing gestures. "It was an error. We had no intention of going in! It was all because of the schottische, you see. The dancing got us quite turned around. And we left at once when we realized where our wrong turn had taken us. I assure you we did not touch any of Lord Fredrick's things." Penelope felt she ought to confess everything, so she added, "Jasper and—"

"*Hush*, Miss Lumley, please!"

"—Margaret were there as well. But if I should see the almanac I will bring it to you at once." This missing almanac business was not nearly as interesting as highwaymen would have been, but at least now it was all settled. Penelope smiled and was about to wish Mrs. Clarke pleasant dreams before snuggling back under the covers.

But Mrs. Clarke seemed suddenly unwell. She clutched at her heart with one hand, leaned against the door, and seemed not to notice how the candle in her other hand had tipped slantwise in its silver holder.

"Take heed, Mrs. Clarke," Penelope said cautiously, "you are likely to drip wax on yourself if you are not careful. That will give a nasty burn."

"Wax!" Mrs. Clarke exclaimed. "Wax, she says! A nasty burn should be the least of my problems. Miss Lumley, you have put me in a pretty pickle, you have. You have opened a can of worms! Now what am I supposed to tell Lord Fredrick? If he looks me in the eye and demands to know what I have discovered, I will have no choice but to tell him what you've told me. I can't lie for toffee, it makes my head ache!"

Mrs. Clarke heaved such agonized sighs, she nearly blew out the flame. Finally, she turned to go, yet she paused in the doorway. "Miss Lumley, do you say your prayers before bedtime, may I ask?"

"Certainly I do," Penelope replied faintly. The notion that perhaps she had offered too much information was only now dawning on her.

"Then I suggest you pray that the blasted almanac is found before morning! Otherwise, I fear that you, and the children—and Jasper and poor Margaret, too!—will be in for a most unpleasant day tomorrow. Good night!"

IF YOU HAVE EVER STAYED UP LATE at night reading a particularly exciting story under the covers with a flashlight, you already know that dramatic events at bedtime do nothing to encourage a restful night's sleep. Penelope tossed and turned for hours, and when morning finally came, for once she did not wish the water in her washbasin even one degree warmer than it was. The brutally cold splash was necessary to wake her and brace for whatever "unpleasantness" might lie ahead.

She did not have to wait long for it to begin; in fact, she had barely made it through the task of giving the children the day's spelling words before the summons came. Margaret's high-pitched voice soared even higher with nervousness as she delivered the message—"Lady Constance requests your presence in the dining room— as soon as you can, she says! Oh my, oh my!"

Penelope had not had a reason to enter the formal dining room of Ashton Place before. "This must be what the great cathedrals of Europe look like!" she thought, as she stared with amazement at the high, beamed ceiling and rows of arching windows. From this you may safely conclude that Penelope had never been inside an actual cathedral, but it was an enormous room nevertheless, the kind in which your voice echoes everywhere if you should somehow muster the courage to speak.

The great mahogany dining table was big enough to fit all the knights of King Arthur's court, although of course it was the wrong shape (King Arthur liked his knights in a circle, while this table was long and rectangular, but still, it was very large). Even Lady Constance seemed to have shrunk a size smaller just by virtue of standing within this vast, imposing space.

An army of servants were scurrying around the table like ants, sorting, counting, and polishing what Penelope was certain must be a mine's worth of silver. Dinner plates, dessert dishes, creamers, skewers, candlesticks, butter dishes, forks, spoons, teapots, trays, platters, ladles, tureens—the long table was covered end-to-end with treasure.

"There you are, Miss Lumley!" Lady Constance trilled as Penelope approached. "And how are your preparations for the party coming along? The children are excited, no doubt? There is so much to do! As you see, today we must take inventory of the silver to see if we are sufficiently stocked to entertain. There is barely enough here for even a medium-sized gathering, but with the purchase of a few new platters and serving spoons, we will muddle through somehow."

"I am well, thank you, and so are the children" was all Penelope could manage in answer.

"Christmas is such a pleasant time of year. And yet so horribly exhausting! Do the children know what to expect of the holiday? The stockings, the caroling, the tree, and so forth? Oh, dear, I suppose I will have to have gifts for them! Motherhood is still so new to me, tra la!"

Now, Penelope did not know what to think. You will recall that she had expected she might be scolded for entering Lord Fredrick's study and perhaps falsely accused of taking the almanac. It had even occurred to her that the police might be summoned and criminal charges filed, after which she would have to bravely defend herself in front of a stern, white-wigged judge. Her eloquence would earn a standing ovation from the dazzled spectators, who would find it impossible to believe that this mere girl of fifteen was not a trained lawyer.

Yet the conversation did not seem to be headed in that direction at all.

"Miss Lumley, you must be wondering why I called for you," Lady Constance said charmingly. "It is because I must apologize!"

Penelope's mouth fell open. "For what?" she tried to say, but the sound got stuck someplace inside her throat.

"Poor Fredrick! He is such a doting and perfect

husband in every conceivable way, but now and then his temper becomes quite excitable." Lady Constance smiled with excessive sweetness. "I expect you have got wind of this almanac business?"

Penelope nodded, afraid to say anything.

Lady Constance's forced laugh echoed through the dining hall. "Dear me, you would think that tattered old book was the family Bible, the way he frets over it! But he says it is important; it has to do with practical matters, scheduling the rotation of the crops and determining the best times of year for trapping badgers and so forth. I don't pretend to understand men's business. Well, when he mentioned at breakfast that it was missing, naturally I replied, quite idly, that perhaps the children were using it. Only because I noticed there are so very many books in the nursery—and really, do you think that is necessary? I worry all that reading will injure their poor eyes! And of course I was thinking back to the sorts of mischief my brothers and I got into when I was a girl. Oh, we were magpies! We would steal Papa's cigars and hide them in the sofa cushions! We were terribly spoiled. I'm sure our old governess would have spanked us if she'd had her own way, but of course she would never dare, my mother would have fired her on the spot. Do you spank the Incorrigibles, I wonder? You may if you like, you know; it wouldn't bother me in the least."

"I have not yet found it necessary," Penelope said, trying to keep her temper steady.

"Really?" Lady Constance seemed surprised. "How curious. In any case, I said what I said without thinking; I assure you I meant no harm by it. But, oh, what a fit my Fredrick threw! 'I rue the day I ever found that grubby lot in the forest,' he roared. Truly, he is not mean or cross as a rule, as I say, just every now and again, when he's been away at his club and then comes home late at night. I think sometimes the whiskey they serve there must give him a headache."

By this point Penelope felt like Longfellow's doomed *Hesperus*, battered to and fro by the relentless storm of Lady Constance's words. Like the brave sea captain's daughter, she knew she must simply endure until it was over.

"But then—oh, I hope you will not think me ridiculous." Lady Constance picked up a silver serving tray and checked her reflection in it before putting it back with the others. "I watched him snort and stamp around the room like an angry bull for a full two minutes before I remembered: I had borrowed the almanac myself!"

"You? So—but—does that mean it is found?" Penelope stammered.

"It was never lost! It was on my dressing table, right where I'd put it." Lady Constance seemed pleased for no good reason that Penelope could comprehend. "It was all because of the party invitations, you see! Naturally I assumed my party would be on Christmas, but the stationer was kind enough to remind me that, out here in the country, it is customary to have an evening party when the moon is full, so that guests can travel safely." She sighed. "Not like London, where you can throw a party whenever you please. I find the gaslights of London thrilling—ah, but you have never seen them? You must. The charms of the city are quite preferable to this rustic life, in my opinion."

There was nothing about the grandeur of Ashton Place that Penelope thought could fairly be called "rustic," but she kept that opinion, along with several others, to herself.

"So the almanac had to be consulted. I meant to put it back where I found it, but then my attention was completely absorbed with choosing the exact shade of paper for the invitations, and the color of ink for the calligrapher, and—well, it just flew out of my head."

Penelope was half dizzy from following the corkscrew turns of Lady Constance's conversation, but at least she was glad to learn that she and the children

135

(and Margaret and Jasper) were safe from any possible accusation. Even so, what was the point of this story? For an awful moment Penelope thought that she might have unwittingly become Lady Constance's confidante. O dreadful fate! Day after day, listening to this endless prattling—she would rather be governess to a whole pack of actual wolves than suffer through that.

"So *that* is why I must apologize," Lady Constance concluded. "For in all the confusion over that silly, silly almanac, I completely forgot to have anyone tell you that I arranged for my dressmaker to come to fit you and that naughty minx, Cassiopeia, for your party dresses. Her name is Madame LePoint." Lady Constance pronounced it in the French manner, so it sounded like "leh pwanh." It was a very ducklike utterance—*pwanh, pwanh, pwanh.* Penelope could imagine how a flock of mallards rising into the air would make that exact sound.

"When is the appointment?"

"Why, today! Madame is here now, waiting in the drawing room. And the tailor is here, too, to measure the boys, although boys' clothes are so much less interesting than girls'. Shall I have Mrs. Clarke escort them to the nursery?"

"No need. I will take them there myself," Penelope said in a daze. She did not wonder that Lord Fredrick occasionally suffered from headaches; ten minutes of conversation with Lady Constance and she was starting to get one herself.

"And it turns out the party will be on Christmas Day, after all!" Lady Constance chirped. "The moon herself insists upon it! Isn't that simply *perfect?*"

As if summoned by Penelope's thoughts of the previous evening, a small package arrived from Miss Charlotte Mortimer in the morning's post. Penelope read the enclosed letter greedily while Madame LePoint measured Cassiopeia for her dress.

My dear Penny,

I am so pleased to hear from you! Your thanks are kind but totally unnecessary; there was nothing in my letter of recommendation but the plain truth. You have earned your position on your merits, and you should be very proud of yourself, as I am.

Your three pupils fascinate me more than I can say; I hope you will send frequent & detailed updates as to their progress. I trust they do not yet speak sufficient English to describe what their life in the forest was like, or what they might remember of life before then?

I hope you will not mind a small piece of advice: Do not

let them run free in the forest. I have reason to think the woods of Ashton Place may hold dangers for them that you cannot anticipate. Call it the intuition of an old teacher!

You must forgive me for a very foolish omission! In my haste to bid you farewell at the station, I forgot to give you the enclosed package. It is a supply of the same herbal poultice used to treat your hair at Swanburne. I strongly recommend you apply it every six weeks, as we have always done.

Be strong, my ha'Penny, and look after your students! Your new life must be very grand indeed, and no doubt you will face many unexpected challenges. But I know you will remain the same brave, clear-eyed, and good-hearted girl you have always been. I look forward to your next letter.

Your friend & fellow educator,
Miss Charlotte Mortimer

Penelope folded the letter with care and slipped it into her pocket. "Silly Miss Mortimer," she thought with a smile, "as if I would let any of my students run free in a wood full of wild animals! She is overcautious to remind me, but I know it is only out of concern."

And it was true that life at Ashton Place was very grand and that most people would consider this a stroke of good fortune, for the children and for Penelope as well. But as she watched poor Cassiopeia endure what was without question a very long fitting for such a short dress (the little girl being only a smidgen over three feet tall), it occurred to Penelope that the simple, unspoiled life at Swanburne might suit most children far better than being forced to stand still for hours while a dressmaker wrapped one 'round and 'round in expensive sateens, sticking terrifying pins here and there and scolding "Don't move, don't move!"

"Cassawoof hot!" the child begged. "Cassawoof no dress!" She looked imploringly at Penelope. The boys had gotten off easy; the tailor had quickly taken their measurements and then left, after announcing that he would be making them each a crisp white-and-blue sailor suit with a black kerchief to tie around the neck. For Madame LePoint, however, mere measurements would not suffice. She had brought dozens of different fabrics with her, plus swatches of ribbon and lace, scissors, boxes of pins, and armloads of taffeta. The pinning had already gone on for hours, and Penelope had run through all the treats in the nursery trying to keep Cassiopeia from squirming loose and hiding under her bed.

"Are you almost done, Madame LePoint? We are eager to get back to our lessons." Penelope tried to sound polite, but she too had lost patience.

"I'll be done when I am done, mademoiselle!"

139

Madame LePoint kept the spare pins pressed between her lips as she worked and, thus, could talk only out of one side of her mouth, but this did not prevent her from speaking rapidly and in a French accent, too. "A party dress is a work of art, no? It takes time. And the little girl has such unusual coloring. Look at her hair: One rarely sees such a rich shade of auburn on a child. I must find the perfect fabric to set it off." She held a swatch of silk next to Cassiopeia's hair. "The moss green suits her beautifully, but this lemon yellow is too much."

Then she held the same swatch against Penelope's hair. "Feh! So drab! Nothing clashes, but nothing matches, either. *Tant pis!*" This was a French expression Penelope understood to mean "too bad, tough luck, that's the way the croissant crumbles," or something along those lines.

"I am sorry that it is beyond your skill to make a dress to flatter my complexion," Penelope said curtly. She was not vain, of course, but that did not mean she did not have feelings. She knew her hair was not particularly striking. It was very dark, nearly black, and lacked shine. That is why Miss Charlotte Mortimer had sent the herbal poultice; at Swanburne her headmistress used to apply it to Penelope's head every six weeks or so to maintain scalp health and repel lice. No doubt it helped, but Penelope had long ago accepted that a thick mane of glossy, bouncy ringlets was not destined to be hers. However, she had read many books in which girls who start out plain blossom into great beauties, and almost as many in which girls who stay plain are loved all the more for their warm hearts and good common sense. Penelope was confident that one fate or the other would be hers eventually, and so she tried not to give the matter too much thought.

Madame LePoint snorted, which was potentially dangerous because of all the pins in her mouth. Happily none of them took flight. "Of course I will make you a dress! You can't attend a holiday ball looking like *that*." The dressmaker jerked her head in the direction of Penelope's plain frock and apron. "Lady Ashton has given me detailed instructions."

"Very well, but I would prefer not to look ridiculous, if you please." There would be no enormous cage crinolines for her, thank you! Penelope was not interested in weaving and bobbing through the party like a birdcage on a luggage trolley. She imagined something more refined, perhaps an off-the-shoulder silk with a gathered bodice and small, tasteful bustle. A shimmery deep blue would suit her well, she thought. She had never owned a garment in such an eye-catching color, but the Swanburne uniform featured a trim of navy ribbon around the hem that Penelope had always found pleasing.

"*Phht! Phht! Phht! Phht!*" One by one, the dressmaker spit her pins back into the box. Cassiopeia took this as her cue to wilt, panting, to the floor. Madame LePoint ignored the child and turned to Penelope. "Don't worry. For you I will make something 'governessy.' That is what Lady Constance has ordered. I have her instructions written on the receipt."

"'Governessy'?" Penelope looked with sudden longing at the sumptuous fabrics arrayed before her. "What could that possibly mean?"

"The dress will be modest and plain. You would not want to be mistaken for one of the guests, after all." Madame LePoint waved another fabric swatch in Penelope's direction and clucked her tongue disapprovingly. "*Alors, alors!* It makes no difference what you wear, really. I'll put you in dark gray. I believe I have some left over from a funeral."

The Tenth Chapter

*Too much shopping leads to an
argument about thespians.*

Extraordinarily busy places are often compared to beehives, and if you have ever seen the inside of a beehive, you already know why this is so.

(It is not necessary to actually set foot inside of a beehive to confirm this, by the way. They are too small and too full of bees for in-person tours to be truly convenient. But there are alternatives: One could peer inside using some sort of periscopelike magnifying device, for example. Or one could simply accept that beehives are busy and get on with it. This second option is called "suspending one's disbelief," and it is by far the easiest row to hoe, now and at other times, too.)

All of which is to say: During the weeks leading up to the party, Ashton Place was an absolute beehive of activity. The cleaning, decorating, and cooking proceeded around the clock. The aroma of baking breads and roasting meats mingled in the air with the scent of the waxes and oils used to polish the woodwork, and the fresh, outdoorsy smell of the pine wreaths and garlands that festooned every available surface. Red velvet ribbons were tied in prettily drooping bows around the balusters of the central staircase and great urns of scarlet poinsettia flanked the doorways. Most impressive to Penelope was the fact that each room had its very own Christmas tree, except for the ballroom, which had two—one on either end.

The actual work was done by the servants, of course, but the queen bee of all this busyness was indisputably Lady Constance. She flew from room to room in a state of nervous excitement that made her even more talkative than usual. Since Lord Ashton's time was devoted to some important business in town, it was Miss Penelope Lumley who increasingly found herself on the receiving end of her mistress's desire to chat.

In fact, Penelope had finally resumed reading "The

Wreck of the Hesperus" to the children, at the very spot where she had been interrupted during her previous attempt:

> *"Colder and louder blew the wind,*
>   *A gale from the Northeast,*
>   *The snow fell hissing in the brine,*
>   *And the billows frothed like yeast."*

—when, unexpected and unannounced, Lady Constance herself dropped by the nursery.

"Good morning, Miss Lumley. And—good morning, children," she added, with a hint of nervousness. Evidently she had not forgotten the licking incident.

With no prompting at all the children sprang to their feet. "Good morning, Lady Constance," they replied, quite nicely.

Lady Constance's golden eyebrows lifted high in surprise. "Well, that is progress! And did I just hear some mention of yeast? Are you reading a cookbook? That would be a very practical thing to study."

The children shook their heads.

"Wreckawoo," Beowulf explained.

"By Longfelloooo," added Alexander.

"Hesperus!" Cassiopeia offered. It came out like a

little bark. "Hesperus! Hesperus!"

"Hmm! How very interesting all that sounds." Lady Constance was clearly bewildered and turned to Penelope. "Miss Lumley, may I speak to you for a moment?" She went on without waiting for a reply. "I am planning a shopping expedition in town tomorrow, and I thought that you—and perhaps the children—might care to join me."

"Arf!" Cass jumped excitedly at the prospect, but Penelope threw her a reproving look.

"Words are better than barks, Cassiopeia," she reminded.

"Cassawoof town, yes!" the little girl corrected herself. The boys also seemed to react positively. Alexander smiled an eager, panting smile, and Beowulf started to drool, which was a sure sign that he found the idea appealing. The drooling was a habit Penelope was slowing training him out of; for now she was relieved Lady Constance seemed not to notice, as she was still prattling away.

". . . Old Timothy can drive us in the new brougham, so there will be plenty of room in the carriage. I have a frightfully long list of things to buy. Of course I *could* send Mrs. Clarke, but then I thought—no, it would be simply too much fun to go shopping! But I can't abide going alone. I have been all but imprisoned in this house for *days* now, with so much to do and the party barely a week away. . . ."

The prospect of a trip to town was exciting to Penelope as well, but a long journey in the carriage with Lady Constance and the Incorrigibles, followed by a tiring day of shopping—would that be wise? She had been working very diligently with the children on good manners, socially useful phrases and appropriate party conversation topics; perhaps this expedition could serve as a valuable rehearsal. And, too, it was the most happy and excited she had seen the children since that awful visit to Lord Fredrick's study.

"Please, Lumawoo?" Alexander tugged at her sleeve.

"Please *please*, Lumawoo?" Beowulf added fervently.

"Lum*ahwoooooo!*" Cassiopeia looked up at her with wide, entreating eyes.

The howling jostled Penelope out of her thoughts. She realized Lady Constance was still waiting for an answer.

"Of course, Lady Constance," she said, flustered. "You are very kind to invite us. It will be our pleasure to accompany you to town."

"Lumawoo?" Lady Constance repeated. There was a curious expression on her face, and she looked at each of the children in turn. "Is that what they call you? How fascinating these Incorrigibles are. I am starting to see my husband's point. It will be terribly amusing to show them off at the party—after all, no one else has anything like them! Tomorrow, then. We shall leave promptly at ten o'clock. What fun we shall have! I am sure I will hardly sleep a wink tonight thinking about it!"

After Lady Constance left, the children were so excited that it took ten full minutes for Penelope to turn their attention back to the fate of the doomed *Hesperus*. Once she did, they were riveted by its tale of a shipwreck in a terrible winter storm at sea. After she reached the tragically thrilling last lines—

"Such was the wreck of the Hesperus,
In the midnight and the snow!
Christ save us all from a death like this,
On the reef of Norman's Woe!"

—the children's appreciative howls of "Norman's *Ahwoooooooooooooe!*" rang throughout the nursery with such convincing mournfulness, Penelope thought that

Longfellow himself would approve.

When Penelope returned to her room that evening, she found a lilac-scented envelope had been slipped under the door. Inside was an impressive sum of cash and a brief note: *Perhaps you will find it convenient to receive a portion of your salary prior to going shopping— with thanks for your service & c., Lady C.*

THE NEXT MORNING'S DEPARTURE went remarkably smoothly. In fact, when the children saw the gleaming carriage with its two horses in harness, they immediately called out "Rainbow! Silky!" and had to be gently dissuaded from braiding the beasts' manes and tails on the spot. They spent the journey looking wide-eyed out the carriage windows. The fact that a strong pane of glass stood safely between them and whatever wildlife they might spot along the side of the road allowed Penelope to concentrate on her knitting in a most relaxed way.

Lady Constance chatted incessantly about all that she planned to buy. Her shopping list for the party even included some items for the children: new gloves for everyone, straw sailor hats for the boys to match their sailor suits, and a small reticule for Cassiopeia (a reticule was a kind of tiny purse; what Cassiopeia might put in it was a mystery to Penelope, but Lady Constance thought her little party outfit would look "ever so much more complete" with the addition of such a bag).

"And I must also keep my eye out for a very special *cadeau,*" she said gaily, "for I have not yet found the perfect gift for my Fredrick. When I am done shopping, I intend to surprise him for an impromptu lunch! Won't he be pleased?"

There was no way for Penelope to know the answer to that question, but Lady Constance did not seem to expect a reply, so Penelope decided it was wisest to say nothing. She had her own thoughts to occupy her in any case. The notion of shopping for presents in a busy town full of stores, with a pocketful of money to spend—this was a type of recreation Penelope had never experienced before, and the prospect made her giddy. She planned to buy presents for the children and Mrs. Clarke, for Miss Charlotte Mortimer, and also for Margaret and Jasper, to thank them for their assistance with the schottische. After some internal debate, she decided she ought to get something for Lady Constance, too. It might be seen as presumptuous, but on the other hand, who didn't like presents?

Lady Constance instructed Old Timothy to drop

them off at the busiest part of town, where all the best (that is to say, most expensive) stores were to be found. He was then to deliver a message to Lord Ashton at his club instructing him to meet Lady Constance for lunch at the Dying Swan Tearoom in two hours' time. At that location they would all rendezvous at four o'clock to return to Ashton Place.

This plan suited Penelope perfectly, for it meant that she would have some time to shop without having to listen to Lady Constance's endless talk. As for the children, she could only hope they would remain reasonably calm. She had brought many treats along as a safety precaution, and the wool for her knitting could always be used as a leash in a pinch. Fortunately, the artificial sights and sounds of the town did not provoke the Incorrigibles in quite the same way that the squirrels of the forest did. Rather than tempt them to run off, the hustle and bustle of the streets made the children cling to Penelope's skirts, and they were visibly relieved when they entered the relative calm of the milliner's shop.

Once there, the boys posed comically in their new sailor hats and thanked Lady Constance profusely by using the socially useful phrases Penelope had taught them, such as "Most appreciated!" and "I offer you my humble gratitude." At first, Cassiopeia was confused by her reticule and started to gnaw on the leather clasp, but Penelope quickly corrected her and all was well.

There was a small bookstore tucked between the milliner's and the shoemaker's shops. Lady Constance had walked past it without a second glance, but Penelope made a mental note to return as soon as Lady Constance left for her lunch appointment. That hour came soon enough, and although she got stuck holding all the packages—"Would you mind terribly, Miss Lumley? I couldn't possibly arrive at the tearoom carrying so many boxes and bags. Fredrick will accuse me of squandering the Ashton family fortune in a single afternoon, and besides, my poor fingers are beginning to ache!"—Penelope was glad to be left to her own devices at last.

"This way, children," she said, leading them straight to the bookstore. "We have some shopping of our own to do." Once inside, she was able to settle her three charges in a corner of the children's section to watch the packages and flip through books. They immediately seized upon a copy of a popular new book that was on prominent display. Beowulf handed it to Penelope so she could see the title.

"Hmph," she said. "It is called *Mayhem for Boys:*

First Lessons in Wanton Destruction."

The children looked at her, confused.

"Mayhem?" Alexander tentatively asked. "Mayhem yes?"

"No! No mayhem, no!" Penelope corrected firmly. "I'm sure it is meant to be ironic."

They looked even more confused. Penelope sighed. Irony was certainly a worthy topic for discussion, but she was eager to start browsing among the books.

"Irony is when you say one thing but mean something else," she explained quickly, "or when you expect things are going to happen one way and then they turn out quite differently—well, it is difficult to put into words. I will have to point out an example when one arises. Now behave yourselves and do not leave this spot. I will return as soon as I have done with my shopping."

Finally, she was free to find presents for everyone on her list. First, the children. For Alexander she chose an introductory Latin text; for Beowulf a collection of Shakespeare's sonnets; and for Cassiopeia a book of Greek myths that explained the tales behind the constellations (including the girl's namesake, the crown-shaped arrangement of stars the Greeks called Cassiopeia, which can easily be seen in the northern sky to this very day). They were ambitious choices, perhaps, but as Agatha Swanburne once said, "When the impossible becomes merely difficult, that's when you know you've won."

She even found something suitable for Lady Constance: a small volume about the stately homes of England that was mostly pictures. Selections were made for Mrs. Clarke (a collection of pudding recipes), Margaret (a popular romance novel that Penelope herself had difficulty putting down once she peeked inside), and Jasper (a thrilling memoir of Arctic exploration by Lieutenant Bedford Pim of the Royal Navy, including his dog-sled encounters with the native Esquimaux people of wildest Canada! Penelope hoped it would not be rude to ask to borrow this volume back once Jasper was done reading it).

Miss Charlotte Mortimer was the most difficult to choose for, as she had already read so many books. Penelope finally settled on a lovely blank journal that she thought would make an elegant gift.

When Penelope paid for all these items and realized she still had enough money left over to stop at the confectioner's for chocolate, she was filled with a rare and wonderful feeling: For the moment at least, her life overflowed with more good fortune than she had previously known existed. Beaming, she went to fetch the children.

"All right, children, I am all done shopping, and now we will have a most delicious surprise. Children?" Penelope looked around the children's section. The packages were heaped in the corner where she had left them. A copy of that ridiculous *Mayhem for Boys* book was lying facedown on the carpet, but the Incorrigibles were gone.

"Alexander? Beowulf? Cassiopeia! Where are you?" Up and down the aisles she searched. They were not admiring the Giddy-Yap, Rainbow! books, nor were they browsing in the poetry section. In desperation she even climbed into the front window display and knocked over the tall stacks of books beneath the New from America sign (the featured title was a shockingly long novel that seemed to be about a whale; it was nearly as heavy as one, too, judging from how it felt when one of them landed on Penelope's foot). But there was no sign of the children, anywhere.

Penelope grew so worried, she started to pant, just as the children would do. What if they had wandered away and were now lost in the city, with its busy, dangerous streets and large, succulent population of pigeons?

"Stop, no, don't come any closer! Stand back,

children, someone will get hurt—"

The old lady's voice was drowned out by a surge of yapping and barking. The noise was coming from outside the store.

Penelope ignored the angry clerk who was scolding her for ruining the window display, pushed through the long line of customers waiting at the cash register, and raced outside to the street. Halfway up the block she saw the three Incorrigibles gathered in a tight circle on the sidewalk. Whatever poor creature they had surrounded was clearly the property of an elderly, fashionably dressed woman who swung her handbag wildly while calling out, "Please, children, keep your distance! Leave my Reginald alone!"

"Alexander Incorrigible!" Penelope barked sternly, as she caught up with them. "What on earth is going on out here? The other two may be forgiven for leaving the bookstore without permission, but you are old enough to know better."

Sheepishly, Alexander stepped back, and his two siblings followed suit. Gazing up at her from the sidewalk was a tiny, sad-eyed Yorkshire terrier. It wore a large, garishly jewel-studded collar.

"Ma'am, I am deeply sorry that the children disturbed you during your walk." Penelope curtsied for

"Leave my Reginald alone!"

extra politeness. "I am their governess. I should not have left them unattended even for a moment."

The woman looked at her with understanding. "No need to apologize, my dear! I was only worried that they might get hurt. My Reginald is not at all friendly, I'm afraid. He nips and bites at the slightest provocation. I can never let anyone get near him for fear they will lose a finger, especially children— Heavens, will you look at that!"

Beowulf was down on his haunches, scratching Reginald gently between the ears and murmuring to him in some mysterious doggie language. The little terrier had a look of pure bliss on his scruffy whiskered face. Soon he rolled over onto his back for more.

"He seems to be in a fine mood now," Penelope observed.

"But—I am shocked! He has never let anyone rub his tummy before," the woman cried.

"Regawoo sad," Beowulf explained. "Neck hurts. See?"

Before anyone could stop him, Beowulf unbuckled the fancy collar that Reginald wore and pressed it hard against the hand of the dog's owner.

"Don't be silly, little boy. This is the special collar I bought when Reginald was just a puppy. He wears it all the time— *Ouch!* It scratched me. How can that be?" She turned the collar over, and a look of realization spread across her face. "The sharp prongs that hold on the jewels are bent outward, rather than in. Oh, how awful! All this time poor Reginald has been suffering, and I had no idea. Come, my darling pooch, let me carry you home. You must never wear that awful collar again."

As soon as the collar came off, Reginald's tail began thrashing side to side with joy. Now he all but leaped into his mistress's arms and covered her face with adoring licks. She looked as if she might cry. "Oh, Reginald! In all our years together you have never shown me such affection! Finally we can be happy. Tonight I shall cook you a nice lamb chop to celebrate. . . ."

As Penelope and the Incorrigibles watched, the woman toddled down the street in happy communion with her canine companion, who now rode contented and collarless in her purse.

"Lamb chop, cooked?" Alexander frowned. "Lamb chop, yuk."

Cassiopeia nodded sagely. "Regawoo ketchup," she said. "Ketchup, ketchup, ketch*awooooooo!*"

THE MINOR DELAY CAUSED BY the encounter with Reginald, the necessity of going back in the bookstore to help the clerk tidy the window display and then gather up all their packages, plus a final stop at the confectioner's—for certainly the children deserved chocolate now!—all conspired to put Penelope and the Incorrigibles somewhat behind schedule. As Penelope was paying for their dark chocolate fudge, their milk chocolate mousse tarts, their chocolate almond toffee, and their chocolate peppermint candy, she glanced at the clock that hung above the counter and realized it was nearly four o'clock.

"Come, children, we must run to meet the carriage right away. It is time!" she cried. Quickly she gathered up all the packages in her sticky hands, and she and the children made their way as best as they could through the holiday crowds, back to the Dying Swan Tearoom where Old Timothy was to meet them. Despite their best efforts they were two minutes late; the carriage was already there, and Lord and Lady Ashton were standing together by the door.

Penelope was so mortified by her tardiness that she ran straight to Lady Constance and blurted half a paragraph of apologies before realizing that the lady and her husband were in the middle of a heated conversation. Even more embarrassed, she crept into the carriage where the children were already busy

gobbling up all the chocolate. Despite her usual misgivings about eavesdropping, she could not help it; she
could hear every word through the carriage window.

"Blast it, Constance, all I'm saying is, this party of
yours—couldn't it be pushed back a few days?"

"Pushed back?" Lady Constance repeated the words
as if they were in a language she did not understand.
"What can that possibly mean?"

"Change the day. Reschedule. Have it the following
week. That's not such a catastrophe, what? Gives you
more time to fuss over the house, too—all your hanging
wreaths and gilt-edged baubles and whatever else you
have planned."

There was a terrifying silence. Then:

"Fredrick. This is a *Christmas* party. It is to be held
on *Christmas Day.* Are you suggesting that I can somehow change the date of Christmas?"

"Now, Constance, don't take it that way—"

"May I also remind you that the invitations have
already been sent, the musicians have been engaged,
the flowers have been ordered? Even the moon is
cooperating! And Leeds' Thespians on Demand have
already been booked!"

"I say, Constance—thespians? Surely that is an
unnecessary expense."

"But they are the *entertainment*!" Lady Constance's voice rose steadily in pitch as she spoke, like an operatic soprano *la-la-la*-ing her way up the scale. "People say their *tableaux vivant* are positively lifelike!"

"Sounds awfully dull for a party, what?" Lord Fredrick chuckled, rather meanly, in Penelope's opinion. It seemed to her that Lady Constance was losing the argument. It must have seemed so to Lady Constance as well, because her childish protests abruptly gave way to a different strategy.

"My dear husband," she said, with an icy calm. "Leeds' Thespians are simply all the rage right now. We are lucky to get them, and I am quite sure they cannot come any other day. The date of the party cannot be changed; it is out of the question. In fact, I am astonished that you would make such an unreasonable request. Why, pray tell?"

Silence. Penelope wondered if Lord Fredrick would press the issue further, and she heard him take in a breath as if to continue the debate—but then he surrendered all at once, like a chess player tipping over his king.

"Sorry to upset the apple cart, dear. You are quite right about the party. Too much trouble to change things about at this late date, and so forth. But unfortunately— that is to say, it's possible"—Lord Ashton hemmed and hawed like a schoolboy who had been called upon by the teacher to provide an answer he did not know—"as a matter of fact, I may have a prior engagement on the day, that's the rub."

Lady Constance gasped audibly. Penelope wondered if there were tears welling up in those round blue eyes.

"What—what sort of engagement could you possibly have on Christmas Day?"

"It is business, dear. It would not interest you."

"But surely it can be changed."

His silence provided answer enough.

"Fredrick, does that mean you will not be attending our party?" She sounded more stunned than angry. "My debut as hostess of Ashton Place? Our first Christmas as husband and wife?"

"Well, I shall do my best. On your way, now; it's getting dark."

"Aren't you traveling back with us in the carriage?"

"I think I shall return to the club for a bit and come home later."

"But we came all this way to meet you! I thought you would ride back home with us."

"Well, I'm sure I never asked you to do that. And don't take those Incorrigible children on any more outings, will you? They might get loose! That would be an awful bother; I'd have to catch 'em all over again. Make sure they're at the party, what? There's a new chap at the club named Quinzy who's itching to meet them, and the fellow's a judge so it's plain common sense to throw him a bone, so to speak. 'A friend on the bench is a friend indeed,' what my father used to say, rest his soul. Now I'll see you after supper, or perhaps a bit later. Up you go, dear.'"

Before any more could be said, Lord Fredrick hoisted his wife into the carriage and nodded to Old Timothy to get under way. Perhaps Penelope imagined it, but it seemed to her that a dark look briefly shadowed the face of the enigmatic old coachman. It was the kind of tense, held-breath expression designed to conceal some strong emotion, like anger, or revulsion, or even fear. But then it was gone, and he called a "Cluck-cluck, heigh-ho!" to the horses, and they were off.

Lady Constance turned her face to the window, away from Penelope. At the moment there seemed nothing Lady-like about her; more than anything she looked like a disappointed young woman who was trying to make the best of a bad hand, a predicament Penelope found easy to understand. For the first time since meeting her, Penelope felt a twinge of compassion for her mistress.

"There are times when married life is not what I expected," Lady Constance finally remarked, after three quarters of an hour had passed.

"I am sorry." Penelope spoke in a soft murmur, so as not to wake the children. By this time all three Incorrigibles had fallen asleep, as children on the way home from a long excursion so often do, even to this day. Their fingers and faces were covered with sticky chocolate, and they lay together all in a heap.

"Oh, don't be sorry!" Lady Constance forced a bitter laugh. "It is only a party, after all. Anyway, I suppose this is what is meant by 'growing up.'"

"Pardon me, my lady—what is?"

Lady Constance smiled tightly, though her eyes shone. "Finding out the difference between what one expected one's life would be like and how things really are."

Penelope found this a thought-provoking remark; it would have served as the very definition of irony if not for the fact that it was so sad—but Lady Constance, rather uncharacteristically, said no more. Other than an occasional sleepy *"Ahwoo"* from a dreaming child, they traveled in silence, through the forest and all its mysteries, back to Ashton Place.

THE ELEVENTH CHAPTER

*Preparations are complete; now
there is nothing to do but pray.*

As YOU MAY HAVE ALREADY had cause to discover, a statement can be both completely true and completely misleading at the same time. This is called "selective truth telling," and it is frequently used in political campaigns, toy advertisements, and other forms of propaganda.

For example, the statement "In the wake of their ill-fated shopping trip, Lady Constance resumed her former distant manner toward Penelope and the children" is a perfectly true sentence that nevertheless fails to paint an accurate picture of events. Lady Constance did resume her former distance toward Penelope and the children, but in fact, she became distant from everyone. She took to her room, had all her meals sent in, and refused to come out, not even to supervise the unpacking of the new crystal champagne flutes that had been special-ordered from a Viennese glassblower and arrived buried in vast crates of sawdust.

Penelope wondered if Lady Constance had taken ill, but when she inquired Mrs. Clarke just rolled her eyes and muttered something about "the moon on a string not being enough for some people." It was an enigmatic reply, but with mere days left before the party Penelope had no time to waste puzzling over how a string might actually be attached to the moon, or whether this was yet another example of poetical language in action.

Instead, during every waking moment from breakfast until bedtime, she drilled the children on all they had learned in preparation for the big event: table manners, proper introductions, handshakes, bows, and curtsies. She tried and quickly abandoned trying to teach them how to play charades; they were simply no good at guessing the names of famous people, since they had never heard of any of them. And she undertook a thorough review of the schottische, making sure to confine the dancing to the nursery this time.

The children endured it patiently and without signs of nervousness, but privately Penelope fretted: What had she forgotten? Was there time to teach Alexander a simple tune on the piano? Cassiopeia might be able to learn a bit of finger crocheting if they worked straight through dinner and used extra thick wool—and Beowulf was very close to being able to do a cartwheel.

But really, how much was too much? It was a party, after all, and parties were meant to be enjoyed. Yet Lord Fredrick had said his friends were "itching" to meet the children; the very idea made Penelope feel as if she might break out in a rash. If the children failed to meet expectations, what then? Every fact and figure Penelope had ever learned seemed to swirl before her eyes. Which skill or scrap of knowledge would be called for? There was no way to tell! She began to panic.

"Remember, children," she said frantically. "Copenhagen is the capital of Denmark! Helsinki is the capital of Finland!"

By this point the children were giddy with fatigue. Alexander nodded gravely and offered a chess piece to his brother.

"Finland?" His voice was comically deep.

"Capital!" Beowulf replied, sounding uncannily like Lord Fredrick.

"Cassawoof poem!" Cassiopeia announced, mischief in her eye. "Title: 'Helsinki':

> "Sinki,
> blinki,
> stinki,
> Helsinki!"

She curtsied, and her brothers dissolved into giggles.

At the sight of the three of them nipping and rolling on the carpet, exhorting each other with socially useful phrases such as "Pass the salt, please!" and "May I take your umbrella?" Penelope realized she had gone too far. They were children; it was Christmas. The party was only a party. They would eat, dance, play, enjoy themselves, and the chips, as they say nowadays, would simply have to fall as they may.

"All right, never mind about Finland." Penelope extended both hands to help the children up from the floor. "As Agatha Swanburne used to say, 'Doing your best is the best you can do,' and we have certainly

The children were quite skilled at identifying
animal tracks in the snow . . .

done our best. Let us take a walk and play outdoors. We have been working too hard for too long, and I believe it has started to snow."

THEIR ROMP OUTDOORS WAS wonderfully invigorating. The children were quite skilled at identifying animal tracks in the snow, although Penelope had to discourage them from actually sniffing their way along the ground. Instead, she taught them to make angels by lying on their backs and waving their arms and legs. They returned to the house in high spirits, with tingling red cheeks and snow-frosted eyelashes. Mrs. Clarke intercepted them at the door.

"There you are! Look at you, all covered with ice like three wild things. By which I mean no offense, of course!" she added quickly.

"No boots in the house!" Alexander said proudly, kicking off his snow-encrusted galoshes. His siblings quickly followed suit.

Penelope flushed with pride at their courteous behavior. What had she been so worried about? The children were charming and well mannered; whatever minor quirks lingered from their unusual upbringing, the howling and drooling and so forth—these would soon fade. She had let herself become fretful for no good reason, and was reminded of how she had foolishly imagined bandits might board the train on the day she arrived at Ashton Place. How easy it was to imagine the worst when one was nervous! And how long ago that fateful day seemed!

She smiled warmly at the housekeeper, whom she now considered a friend. "Never fear, Mrs. Clarke, we shall be very careful not to track snow indoors. I know how hard the staff has worked to make the house sparkle for the party tomorrow."

Mrs. Clarke rolled her eyes. "Oh, the party, the party, it'll be the death of me! It's an awful thing to say of Christmas Day, but the sooner it's over, the better I'll feel. Heavens to Betsy, I almost forgot why I've been standing here waiting for you lot! Lady Constance has come out of hiding, and she's asking for you. I told her you'd gone out-of-doors, and she said very well, but I must tell her the minute you and the children are returned. She wants you to meet with her in the drawing room as soon as you're ready."

Penelope felt the healthy glow she had acquired during their snowy adventure drain from her cheeks. But before she could ask why they had been called, Mrs. Clarke provided the answer.

"My lady says tomorrow she will simply be too

busy, what with the guests arriving and having to get dressed and so forth—so she wishes to give the Incorrigibles their Christmas presents tonight and have it done with."

The children squealed happily at this news. Penelope was relieved and thanked Mrs. Clarke for the information. But privately she thought it was a very questionable practice to give Christmas gifts early; in fact, the idea of it caused her a little pang. Any gift ought to be appreciated, of course, and thank-you notes promptly written, but still—early presents meant there would be that much less to open under the tree on Christmas morning.

Yet, she told herself, the children would be unlikely to mind. To get presents at all must be a novelty to them, and of course they had lived under trees all their lives. It was Penelope herself who liked getting presents on Christmas morning, or if not *presents*, then at least *a present*. Back at Swanburne, at Christmas, each girl was given the task of being a "Secret Swanburne Santa" whose job it was to make something for one of her classmates (all presents had to be handmade, that was the rule). Countless knitted hats, monogrammed handkerchiefs, and needlepoint pillows featuring the sayings of Agatha Swanburne were exchanged annually, but one year Penelope had the good fortune of getting Miss Charlotte Mortimer as her Secret Swanburne Santa, and that was the year she had been given her poetry book.

"But, Miss Mortimer, I thought the gifts had to be handmade," a much younger Penelope had asked, while experiencing a shiver of delight at how completely and thrillingly store-bought the book appeared to be.

"Indeed—and what could be more handmade than a poem?" Miss Mortimer had replied, with a warm and mysterious smile. "That it gets printed in a book after the poet makes it is quite beside the point." This memory was both happy and sad: happy because it was so pleasant, and sad because it made Penelope think about how much she missed Swanburne—the girls, the teachers, Miss Mortimer. Or perhaps it was her own much younger self, that pint-sized person whom she could never be again, whom she missed. It was hard to say.

Then she looked at the three upturned faces of the Incorrigibles, now bright-eyed with eagerness: proud Alexander, dreamy, drooly Beowulf, and clever little Cassiopeia, who was finding it difficult not to pant with excitement for her present. Penelope thought how dear to her they had already become and how much they needed her, and she felt a new source of happiness bubbling up from within, warm and slightly gooey, like the heated chocolate syrup one might pour over an ice cream sundae.

In this way Penelope's happy and sad feelings got all mixed up together, until they were not unlike one of those delicious cookies they have nowadays, the ones with a flat circle of sugary cream sandwiched between two chocolate-flavored wafers. In her heart she felt a soft, hidden core of sweet melancholy nestled inside crisp outer layers of joy, and if that is not the very sensation most people feel at some point or other during the holidays, then one would be hard pressed to say what is.

PLAYING IN THE SNOW even for a short while makes most children ravenously hungry. Judging from the way the Incorrigibles were starting to chew on their mittens, they too were ready for a snack. So, despite the enticement of the presents that awaited them, Penelope first took the children up to the nursery to change into dry clothes and eat a quick supper. Then, after a thorough check to see that their shoes were tied, their hair was combed, and their fingernails were perfectly clean,

Penelope sent word that she would now bring the children down to the drawing room, where they would remain until it was convenient for Lady Constance to receive them.

The drawing room was so warm! There was a fire blazing in the hearth; the flames leaped up in long orange tongues, and the logs crackled and sputtered. Each of the hundreds of shiny baubles that hung on the tall Christmas tree caught the flickering light of the fire and reflected it in miniature, until the tree itself seemed to shimmer and glow. The children stared in awe. Penelope wondered what, if anything, in the mysterious woods they once inhabited could have prepared them for this sight. A meteor shower, perhaps? A forest fire?

"Don't you think the tree is pretty? Really, is there anything as pretty as a Christmas tree? I think it is the prettiest, prettiest thing in the world!"

Lady Constance swept into the room as giddy and foolish as ever; to look at her, you would think nothing unpleasant had ever happened in the whole history of England. She clasped her hands together and spoke with the kind of false, high-pitched cheerfulness adults sometimes feel compelled to use when talking to children. "When I was a little girl, I used to *insist* on sleeping under the Christmas tree on Christmas Eve! I wanted to catch Father Christmas in the act. Wasn't that ever so naughty of me?"

To the Incorrigibles, sleeping under a tree was not, as they say nowadays, a big deal. But they smiled and agreed with what Lady Constance had said.

"You are very kind to think of gifts for the children," Penelope remarked. She did not expect any gift for herself, of course, but the book about stately homes she had selected for Lady Constance was tucked in her apron pocket, wrapped in colorful paper, and sealed with a red ribbon bow. She hoped the perfect opportunity to present it would naturally arise at some point during the conversation.

"I will be frank. I really had no idea what to get you three, but then I thought back to when I was a girl, and the sorts of things my brothers and I would be given as presents, and there you have it." She handed a package to Alexander. "Here, this is for you two boys to share." She produced another package and held it out to Cassiopeia. "And this is for you."

The packages were wrapped perfectly—too perfectly, the way packages are done up when they have been wrapped by a nameless clerk in a store. Possibly because there were two of them tearing away at the paper, the boys managed to get their present opened first.

"What is it? Let me see!" Penelope was excited in spite herself. But the boys looked ashen. With shaking hands, Alexander held up a disturbingly lifelike toy rifle.

"How my brothers loved their guns!" Lady Constance chirped. "That one is only a toy, of course. But perhaps someday you will want real ones."

All Penelope could think of was what it must have been like that day in the forest: three terrified children staring down the muzzle of Lord Fredrick's hunting rifle—the trigger pulled back with a click—Old Timothy intervening at the last minute—

Beowulf gnawed anxiously on his knuckles. Alexander held the toy between two fingers, as if it burned his skin to touch it.

Quickly, Penelope turned to Cassiopeia, who had just succeeded in tearing the ribbon off her present with her teeth. "And what is your present, dear?" she said, trying to inject some light-heartedness back into the proceedings. "It looks like a book, how wonderful!"

Cassiopeia held the book forward. With a sinking heart, Penelope read, "It is called *The Girls' Guide to Obedience and Quietness.*"

"Ironic?" Cassiopeia sounded hopeful.

Penelope sneaked a glance at the giver of these strangely off-putting gifts. In the changeable light of the fire Lady Constance's face seemed an inscrutable, doll-like mask, with half-smiling lips painted on and expressionless glass eyes—all at once Penelope thought the lady bore an uncomfortable resemblance to the animals in Lord Fredrick's study.

The image of Lady Constance's stuffed head mounted on the wall was disturbing and difficult to shake off. "I am not entirely sure about that, Cassiopeia," Penelope finally answered. This was another example of selective truth telling, for although what Penelope said was technically true—she could not be entirely sure what the author's intentions were in terms of irony; the answers to literary questions of this sort are rarely cut and dried, as authors themselves are often at a loss to explain their own intentions—it was also true that she did not like these presents one bit. Lady Constance's weirdly taxidermic facial expression was getting on her nerves, and all her previously laid-to-rest fears about the party had been brought back to life and now lurched terrifyingly around her mind, like Frankenstein's monster.

"There you have it, children," Lady Constance said, with a frozen smile. "Those are your presents. Now I do hope you are going to say thank you!"

Quite without warning, Cassiopeia snarled and bared her teeth.

"Why, whatever is the matter with her? Is she about to attack?" Shielding her face with her hands, Lady Constance shrank back in fear.

Penelope seized Cassiopeia by the arm. "Now, stop that, Cassiopeia! Stop it at once."

Slowly Cassiopeia let her lips unfurl to their usual position, but there was a hard and unrepentant look in her eye. She stared at Lady Constance without blinking.

"These children—are they really savage beasts at heart?" Lady Constance gasped and hid behind an armchair. "Are they dangerous?"

"Hardly! Lady Constance, I am deeply sorry for Cassiopeia's outburst. I am sure she is as well." Unseen, she gave the girl's wrist a sharp squeeze.

"*Ow!* Sorry," Cassiopeia mumbled. "Cassawoof no teeth, no bite, sorry, sorry, sorry."

The boys looked contrite as well, although they had done nothing wrong. "You will excuse me," Beowulf intoned. It was one of the socially useful phrases Penelope had made the children practice. Evidently he was trying to do his part to smooth things over.

"Apologies all around," Alexander said, and then for

good measure he added, "I extend my deepest condolences." It was not quite the right occasion for the remark, but Penelope thought the children's sincerity was clear. However, Lady Constance still looked terrified.

"Listen to that! They do everything together, don't they?" Lady Constance said under her breath. "They are not like siblings at all—they are more like a pack!"

"Cassiopeia is tired from being kept too long out-of-doors in the cold weather. That is my fault." Penelope knew she needed to make an exit, as quickly as possible. "With your permission we shall take our leave, and I will tuck the children straight into bed."

"I'm sure you know best how to manage these creatures," Lady Constance said coolly. "But I warn you, Miss Lumley! If they behave like wild animals at my party tomorrow, I will implore my husband to set them loose in the woods again, where they belong!"

Penelope curtsied and quickly herded the children to the door. In her pocket the wrapped *Stately Homes of England* suddenly felt as if it weighed as much as the houses it depicted, but in her pocket it would have to remain. She knew there was no chance of it receiving a suitable welcome now.

The Twelfth Chapter

*After an anxious wait, the
festivities begin.*

PENELOPE DREAMED OF PRESENTS and awoke thinking
how a nice hand-monogrammed handkerchief always
makes a welcome and appropriate gift. Then she opened
her eyes and remembered what day it was.

"Oh! Christmas!" she exclaimed aloud, and not in
the festive manner one might expect. Today was the
party. If it were a catastrophe, it would be her fault—
and then what would become of them all?

She washed and dressed at twice her customary speed.
By the time she arrived at the nursery, Penelope felt weak

in the knees, and her hands were shaky. It was no way to begin the day, and certainly no way for a Swanburne girl to react under pressure, but no matter how many deep breaths she took or how many times she repeated to herself, "No hopeless case is truly without hope," she could not get her heartbeat to slow its anxious flutter.

In the nursery the children seemed subdued and distracted, as if waiting for something bad to happen. Cassiopeia sat by the window, idly flicking the beads on the abacus up and down. She looked contrite, but Penelope noticed that she had tossed her new book in a corner and had not bothered to pick it up. The boys hovered nearby, shuffling their feet; the toy rifle was nowhere to be seen. Breakfast had been brought in and placed on the table in an elegant silver chafing dish. Penelope lifted the lid and peeked underneath: oatmeal, same as always. Even at Swanburne the girls would get cinnamon toast and sausage on holidays.

"I see that breakfast has not yet been touched," Penelope commented.

"Tummy ache," Beowulf said in a whimper. The other two nodded. There was a sense of anxiety in the air. Penelope knew she had to do something, or the day would be ruined before it had even begun.

"If you please," she said, summoning her calmest

tone, "would someone bring me my copy of *Edith-Anne Gets a Pony*? It is on the bookshelf, in its usual place." She could think of no better antidote for the dark mood of the children; besides, turning her mind to the adventures of that lovable pony was likely to settle her nerves as well.

The children must have been of a similar opinion, for they raced one another to fetch the book. Penelope read aloud while the children squatted on their haunches and listened (normally she would have reminded them to sit in chairs, but she was trying to comfort them after all). After a while they acted out their favorite scenes from the story. It was all very soothing, and as soon as the fog of worry dissipated, everyone's normal hearty breakfast appetites returned, including Penelope's.

It was only when they were done eating that Penelope remembered: Her presents for the children were still waiting, carefully stacked under the small Christmas tree of the nursery!

"Why, children!" she exclaimed, wiping her lips on one of the pressed linen napkins. "Did you neglect to look under the tree this morning? There are more presents for you!"

At the word *presents* they flinched, but Penelope gently guided them to the tree and pointed underneath.

"They are from me," she added softly, and then the children smiled.

How different this moment of gift giving was from that of the previous evening! These presents were chosen with the children's own likes and dislikes in mind, by someone who had their best interests at heart and who had lovingly (although imperfectly) wrapped them herself. The children opened the packages with the appropriate sense of wonder and spent the morning happily leafing through their new treasures, which of course Penelope promised to read to them at her earliest opportunity. When Alexander understood that his Latin book was a primer, he straightaway pretended to be "Miss Lumawoo" teaching Latin to his siblings, and there was much laughter.

As the children played, Penelope retreated to the back nursery and laid out all their fine new clothes, which had been delivered the previous day and were now hanging in the closets under covers of white muslin. This afternoon the party guests would start to arrive. Then it would be time to get dressed and face the music, so to speak, but not yet. She looked out the window. A light snow still fell, blanketing over all tracks and footprints from the previous day.

"That is what we must do as well," Penelope thought.

"Start afresh. There is no need to carry yesterday's fears and disappointments into a brand-new day—especially on Christmas!"

The thought pleased her, so much so that she wondered if it might be some obscure saying of Agatha Swanburne's that she had heard in passing long ago and then forgotten. "But it is not," she realized, with a flush of pride. "In fact, I think it may well be the first memorable saying of Penelope Lumley!"

IT WAS LATE IN THE AFTERNOON when the first guests started to arrive. The Incorrigibles stood with their three noses pressed to the glass of the nursery windows, watching as the carriages pulled up. The grand ladies and gentlemen emerged with the aid of their coachmen, and their luggage was removed and brought inside (in those days it was expected that one would bring luggage for a party, for of course the ladies would have to change before dinner, and then again before the dancing commenced).

Darkness came early, as it always does in December, but the pageant of arriving revelers continued. The moon was full and so bright that the trees cast long blue shadows along the ground; the unearthly glow glittered like diamond dust on the freshly fallen snow. Inside, the house hummed with activity; soon the din of voices was loud enough to carry up to the nursery. Women gaily called to one another, men bellowed greetings and clapped one another on the back. There was a constant scurry of servants racing up and down the halls, tending the fires, hanging up cloaks, putting away umbrellas, and delivering trays of tea to warm the travelers. The ladies were shown to their rooms to rest and change clothes, while the men retreated to the smoking parlor to puff on cigars and talk about taxes, wars, cricket, and other subjects vital to the health of the nation.

"Yes, party!" Cassiopeia cried, no longer able to contain her excitement. "Party now, Cassawoof dress now, now now *now!*" The boys were also much too agitated to do anything but get ready, so finally Penelope gave the children leave to put on their new clothes, although she uttered all the usual cautions about not getting dirty or wrinkled before anyone had had a chance to see them.

Penelope also had to get changed. Her new gray gown had been delivered the previous day along with the children's clothes and was now hanging in the closet of her bedroom. The style of the garment was not what she herself would have chosen, yet she was forced to admit, she was eager to know what it would feel like to wear a brand-new dress, made especially for her by an expensive seamstress with a French accent. That was something she had never experienced before, and (in principle at least) Penelope was in favor of new experiences, as long as they did not upset the digestion.

No sooner did she think of her dress than one of the housemaids, a short and plain-spoken girl whom everyone called Susan, came by the nursery with a message. "A very happy Christmas to you, Miss Lumley—you'd best go get changed now. Mrs. Clarke says you are to come downstairs as soon as you are ready. You and the children are to wait quietly in the ballroom in an out-of-the-way spot until the guests come in from dinner. Lady Constance will introduce you at the proper time."

"My heavens!" Mrs. Clarke exclaimed. "I am sure I have never seen three such extraordinarily handsome and well-turned-out children!"

As you may know, complimentary remarks of this type are all too often made by well-meaning adults to children who are, to be frank, perfectly ordinary-looking. This practice of overstating the case is called *hyperbole.* Hyperbole is usually harmless, but in some cases it has been known to precipitate unnecessary wars as well as a painful gaseous condition called *stock market bubbles.* For safety's sake, then, hyperbole should be used with restraint and only by those with the proper literary training.

However, in this particular instance, Mrs. Clarke's enthusiasm was justified. The boys were dashing in their crisp, new sailor suits, and the addition of the straw hats provided the perfect finishing touch. And Cassiopeia's dress was a marvel—a rich green velvet with exquisite silk rosettes stitched around the bodice. With her delicate frame, thick auburn hair, and wide green eyes, she looked like a woodland pixie from a storybook. Even Penelope had to admit that the clothes were well worth the trouble the tailor and Madame LePoint had put them all to.

Mrs. Clarke was also rather well turned out for the party, in her fashion. The dress she wore was a voluminous mélange of floral patterns that did much to accentuate the impressive girth of the wearer. She resembled nothing so much as a spring meadow in full bloom, depicted at nearly life-size.

As for Penelope, her dress was both dark and gray, and the cut was modest; one might even call it severe. But it was exquisitely made and had been hand-tailored to her exact measurements; she had never worn anything that fit so well. After examining herself in the mirror from every angle she could manage without pulling a muscle, Penelope concluded that she was pleased. The dress made her look older and even a bit forbidding. Wearing it gave her more rather than less confidence, and that is precisely what a well-chosen outfit ought to do.

"And tonight, especially," she thought, as she took a deep breath and followed the children and Mrs. Clarke into the great ballroom, to wait as instructed and then to enjoy whatever festivities the evening had in store for them, "a bit of extra self-confidence is sure to come in useful."

AT SWANBURNE THERE WERE STUDENTS, and there were teachers, and there was Miss Charlotte Mortimer, the headmistress. The pecking order was simple: Students obeyed teachers, and everyone obeyed Miss Mortimer.

But apparently there were a great many more types of people in the world than Penelope had previously realized. The parade of guests into the ballroom was carefully sorted in order of importance. First came the people with actual inherited titles, such as baron or viscount; then came the wealthy landowners, and then the prosperous businessmen. It was all very confusing. Penelope was left with the impression that titles were more important than profession and land was more important than business, but money was far more important than any other sort of accomplishment.

"See, that's the Baron of Whatsit," Mrs. Clarke whispered in her ear. "And there's Countess Whoosis, she's the wife of the Earl of Somewhere or Other. That's Judge So-and-So. And there go Lord and Lady Moneybags; they've been traveling on the continent for a year and only just returned."

Actually Mrs. Clarke was well able to remember most of the actual names, but once the information entered Penelope's head it dissolved into gibberish. She could not think about names; she was too distracted by the glorious gowns the women wore, the elegant way they carried their fans, the colorful headpieces that perched on their heads like pet cockatoos. Only in magazines had she ever seen anything like the bejeweled necks and bare shoulders of these elegant women, with their elaborate upswept hairdos—suddenly, Penelope was ashamed at her own high-collared gray wool dress and her drab dark hair pulled back in a low, simple bun against her neck. The abundant self-confidence she felt while in her room had shrunk to the size of an acorn now that she was really here. She ransacked her memory for some bolstering saying of Agatha Swanburne's—something about vain plumage, perhaps?—but came up empty.

The Incorrigibles just stood there, wide-eyed and trembling. Soon Mrs. Clarke had to leave to give instructions to the waiters, who were now bringing in the tea and after-dinner sweets. Wordlessly, Penelope and the children inched backward until they were almost completely shielded by the tall potted ferns that flanked the entryway (even in her current nervous state Penelope recognized them as Mineola ferns, native to a long island whose name she could not quite recall).

The party guests streamed into the ballroom, but they took no notice of Penelope and the children. For the most part their conversations were barely worth eavesdropping on: "Wonderful dinner! Isn't it grand when it snows on Christmas! What a moon there is tonight, you can see as clear as day out there!" Although once Penelope could have sworn she heard someone say, "And where are these famous savages, I wonder? Locked in cages no doubt! Anybody seen Ashton? Where the devil can he be?"

At last, a bulbous-nosed man spotted them and walked over with another gentleman. He stood in front of Cassiopeia, but he spoke to his companion. "I say, Maytag, look at this charming creature disguised as a houseplant. Do you suppose this is one of the wild children Ashton spoke of at the club? It must be—look, here are the other two, hiding in the ferns."

"Disappointing if so," the other man commented. "They don't seem so very wild at the moment."

"No, ha! They look quite vegetative, in fact." The first man regarded them openly, as if they could not see him examining them from three feet away. "Actually they seem like three unwilling children who've been dressed up and dragged to a party when they'd rather be jumping rope, ha! I quite sympathize." He bent over to put his face quite near to Cassiopeia and spoke loudly and slowly, as if she were an idiot. "Halloo, there, young lady. I am Baron Hoover. And what name do you go by?"

"My name Cassawoof," she said, staring stubbornly at the floor.

"Cassa—what? Woof? Ha, that's rich!" He straightened. "And how about you lads? Do you have woofy names also?"

"Alexander. Pleased to make your acquaintance," Alexander said carefully, with a bow.

"A pleasure, I'm sure—oops! Start over, sorry. Beowulf. A pleasure, I'm sure." Chagrined by his minor muddle, Beowulf cast a nervous glance toward Penelope, who nodded reassuringly.

The man called Maytag looked startled. "Did you

hear that, Hoover? Blast it all, they can talk English, and they're not even covered with hair. Let's go find Ashton and give him a what-for. The chap's been pulling our leg."

Hoover surveyed the children with curiosity. "I'd say you're right, Maytag. Why, these children are perfectly normal, as children go, anyway."

"Bad news, what?" Maytag remarked, as they walked away, drinks in hand. "I expect there'll be no hunting tonight after all."

No hunting tonight . . . What on earth did he mean by that? Penelope felt an icy chill pierce her through. Luckily, the children did not hear this perplexing remark; they were too busy staring at the regal woman with the elaborate fur-collared dress who had just entered the room. One side of the collar was adorned with tails, the other with heads. One would be hard-pressed to pick which side was the lucky one, since both were equally dead.

When Lady Constance made her entrance, she looked like nothing so much as the star attraction of a dessert cart in a fancy restaurant—cream skin, strawberry lips, with her yellow hair swirled 'round her head like rich lemon-butter frosting. Her gown was of the purest white, with a lace overlay that floated around her like mist, nearly invisible except for where it was touched here and there with iridescent beads that glittered as she walked. She was escorted by two different gentlemen, neither of whom was her husband. Her talk was animated, her eyes flashed, her smile dazzled. It was all a bit much. She reminded Penelope of a windup toy whose key has been given a few turns too many.

"I must say, life at Ashton Place has me *completely* spoiled. From the first day it has been a dream come true, and all thanks to my darling Fredrick. And I am sure that was the best dinner I have ever eaten in my life! Now I will have no appetite for normal everyday meals ever again. Next time you see me, I will have wasted away to skin and bones—oh, look who is lurking here among the foliage! It is the legendary, world-famous Incorrigibles and their obscure governess."

Her smile hardly altered, which is to say it did alter, slightly. Something brittle and false seeped into her expression. "Good evening, Miss Lumley. I hope your ears have not been burning! It appears that Lord Fredrick has told his friends at the club a great deal about the children. Indeed, all during dinner some of our guests could hardly speak of anything else. You can imagine how delighted I was about that!"

Clearly Lady Constance was not delighted about it at all; in fact, the mistress of Ashton Place looked as if she might like to punch someone. Penelope readied herself to leap to the children's defense should it prove necessary.

"Now step forward, please, and let me see if the tailor and Madame LePoint have managed to make a silk purse out of a wolf's ear, *ha ha ha!*" The gentlemen at Lady Constance's elbows laughed along obediently. "Hmm, the children are presentable, that is as it should be." She gazed coolly at Penelope. "And Miss Lumley, may I say that dress makes you look positively professional. But, come, you cannot spend the party at the door. Join us for some tea and petites madeleines, and then we shall clear away the dessert tables and the games and the dancing can begin." She leaned close and lowered her voice. "Many eyes will be upon you, Miss Lumley, so take care. You need not speak to anyone unless spoken to, of course."

Penelope tried to work up the courage to ask Lady Constance about this hunting business that the gentlemen had remarked about, but before she could speak, a new admirer was upon them, flanked by Hoover and Maytag. He was older than the other two men, and to be frank he was very ugly to look upon: His hair was coarse and jet-black, his nose was oddly shapeless, and he wore large thick glasses that distorted the shape of his eyes. But his walk had an energetic, feline spring, and there was a disarming, self-mocking lilt to his voice.

"Lady Ashton, you are a vision," he crooned, taking one of her hands in both of his and bestowing upon it a gentlemanly kiss. "That dress suits you. It is like moonlight on snow. And the party is a triumph. It is a shame Lord Ashton could not join us for dinner, of course, but you must not let that trouble you. Be thankful he is not a navy man! Then he would be away from home for months at a time."

At the mention of her husband Lady Constance's left eye began to twitch. "You are very kind, Judge Quinzy. I doubt I should like being married to a sailor, though. I get terribly seasick. One time, when I was a girl, I was just sitting on the riverbank watching a sculling match, and after only a few minutes, I was nearly ready to—"

"Judge Quinzy," Beowulf volunteered, now feeling surer of himself. "Pleased to make your acquaintance."

Judge Quinzy turned to locate the source of this voice emanating from the potted plants. The change in his demeanor upon seeing the children was hard to describe. It was not a change of expression, nor of complexion—it was more as if a sheer curtain had suddenly been drawn across his face.

Baron Hoover nudged Judge Quinzy in the ribs. "'Pleased to make your acquaintance,' did you hear that? Ashton's been putting one over on us. These brats talk better than most of the unwashed hordes that appear before your bench, and the law insists on calling that lot human, doesn't it?"

"It does, Hoover, it certainly does—although not without controversy, in some circles. My, my! So these are the Incorrigible children. Indeed, I was expecting something far more savage. On the other hand, appearances can be deceiving." He regarded them slowly and methodically, one after another. "How fascinating it is to finally meet you. Come, you—all three of you—you must sit at my table for dessert. You cannot refuse; you are without question the most interesting guests at this party, and I intend to get to know you much, much better."

Cassiopeia clutched Penelope's hand tightly. "No Lumawoo?" she asked tremulously. Judge Quinzy looked at Penelope as if he were seeing her for the first time, although of course she had been standing there all along.

"Who's this, then? The governess?" There was a sudden edge to his voice. "Can't she speak?"

Maytag was quite beside himself with chuckling. "Ha! Perhaps Ashton got it all wrong! Perhaps she's the one they found howling in the woods!"

Penelope felt her cheeks flush. If only this fancy gray dress had a nice loose pocket in front for her poetry book! It would have been a comfort to have close by, but even the thought of it was enough to remind her what to do.

"I am Miss Penelope Lumley," she said boldly, with the full force of her education behind her. "I am a graduate of the Swanburne Academy for Poor Bright Females, currently employed as governess here at Ashton Place." Then she looked Judge Quinzy straight in the eye, exactly as if they were equals, for she was a Swanburne girl after all. "It would be our pleasure to consent to join you for dessert."

The twitching in Lady Constance's eye had increased dramatically during this exchange. Now she covered the eye with one hand and excused herself by saying, "Pardon me, I do think a cinder may have flown into my eye—I shall return momentarily—do not forget the petites madeleines!—Margaret, Margaret, oh, will someone ring for my lady's maid, please—?" Then, like a bird with one broken wing, she spun in half-blind circles until someone assisted her to the door.

Judge Quinzy hardly acknowledged Lady Constance's comical exit; his attention was fixed on

Penelope. "Swanburne Academy, eh? I don't believe I've heard of that school; you must tell me all about it. But from the obvious high quality of its graduates—the one I've met so far, at least—I would wager that it's a very worthy institution, very worthy indeed."

This odd compliment made Penelope uncomfortable, although she was not sure why. Then Judge Quinzy offered her his arm, just as he might to one of the fine ladies at the party. What else could she do but take it?

Still holding Cassiopeia's hand tightly with her free hand, Penelope allowed the judge to lead her to his table, with Alexander and Beowulf following close behind. She was careful to keep her gaze straight ahead as they walked. If there happened to be any mocking smiles on the faces of the society ladies as she was paraded across the room on the arm of a judge, it was none of her concern, thank you very much!

Still, though she was too proud to look to see if she were right, she had the unmistakable feeling that every eye in the room was upon her—and upon the children, too.

The Thirteenth Chapter

*Alas, the party does not go
precisely as planned.*

In Miss Penelope Lumley's day it was often said that the mark of a good servant was to do his or her job with brisk efficiency while at the same time remaining "invisible." You may take this as another example of hyperbole, for in Miss Penelope Lumley's day servants did not actually have the power to become invisible, although it certainly would be interesting if they had. (Some years later, a Mr. H. G. Wells would write a definitive book on the subject of invisibility, which is well worth reading. However, under no circumstances are you to repeat the experiments he describes except under the strictest adult supervision.)

Nevertheless, in the very same room and during the same interval of time in which the events of the previous chapter were taking place (that is, the dinner guests entering the ballroom, Hoover and Maytag chatting with the children, Lady Constance's overwound entrance, the odd conversation with Judge Quinzy, and so forth), the servants had been busily (one may even say "invisibly") setting out heaping platters of petites madeleines on the linen-draped tables that ringed the dance floor. Trays of colorful fruit tarts and sweet puddings dusted with a fairy-frost of sugar had also appeared, along with steaming pots of fragrant tea.

Judge Quinzy led Penelope and the children to his table and pulled out a chair. Penelope almost sat down in the one next to it before she realized that he was holding the chair out for her. Alexander, Beowulf, and Cassiopeia sat across from her, along with the Earl of Maytag, Baron Hoover, and a woman whom Penelope quickly identified as the baroness due to the way she scowled at the baron. (Baroness Hoover's nose, Penelope could not help noticing, was as long and sharp as her husband's was broad and bulbous; she thought it would be amusing to imagine them switched, as if they were detachable accessories of the sort one might nowadays see on, say, a vacuum cleaner.)

All counted that made eight at the table; there were still two empty chairs. From across the room Penelope spotted Lady Constance tottering her way back toward them. Even from a distance she looked woefully unsteady. Clearly the stress of Lord Fredrick's absence was wearing on her; for everyone's sake Penelope hoped the tenth chair did not remain vacant much longer.

The men sprang to their feet as Lady Constance approached. "How is your dear little eye, my lady?" asked the Earl of Maytag. "Did you find that wicked cinder? Has the intruder been removed?" Indeed, one of Lady Constance's eyes was now quite red and puffy from being rubbed; the other seemed glazed in the manner of a person who has overindulged in champagne or some similar beverage.

"Thank you for your conshern, shir. There was no shinder; I just sheem to have developed a shilly old twitch." No sooner did she say "twitch" than her eye demonstrated. "I have taken a few ships of a—*hic!*—medishinal cordial that should shoothe the shpasm, shoon enough."

It was obvious that Lady Constance was making

every effort to maintain her dignity, not to mention her balance, but when the Earl of Maytag attempted to push her chair in, she slid off and landed underneath the table with a thud. The men fished her out, but the episode prompted a fit of giggling, which continued until tears streamed down the poor lady's face. In the end she had to put her head down on her dessert dish to recover under the privacy of a large linen napkin, which she pulled over her head like a blanket. The occasional hiccup soon gave way to a soft snore.

The children observed Lady Constance with fascination. In other circumstances Penelope would have pointed out how, finally, here was a perfect example of irony at work: Lady Constance had haughtily predicted that the Incorrigibles would act like wild animals at the party, but it turned out that she was the one whose behavior left something to be desired. However, Penelope could not think of a way to bring up the subject that would not be awkward; with regret she let the moment pass.

In fact, none of the adults knew quite what to say. The table was at serious risk of suffering that social calamity known as the "awkward silence." Luckily, the children had been well trained in the art of party conversation.

"Merry Christmas!" said Alexander to Baroness Hoover. "I do not believe we have been introduced."

"Lovely weather," Beowulf added, carefully selecting a little shell-shaped cake from the tray.

Cassiopeia grabbed one as well and shoved it gleefully in her mouth. "Condolences," she said as an afterthought, but through all the crumbs and chewing, no one could understand her, which was just as well.

"Swallow before conversing, dear," Penelope reminded gently.

Lady Constance let out another snore, which everyone politely ignored. With the precision of a chemist, Baroness Hoover dropped three cubes of sugar into her tea. "So these are the infamous wolf children. You are fortunate"—*plop!*—"that the Ashtons"—*plop!*—"have taken you in. Most wretched waifs"—*plop!*—"in your circumstances would be sent away— *Ouch!* Percy, beloved, why are you kicking me? Have you mistaken me for a chair leg?"

"Apologies, dear heart, but honestly—'wretched waifs'? It's not a nice thing to say at Christmas."

"I am merely being frank. I don't believe in sugarcoating things for the young. That is how I was raised, and I turned out perfectly well." She sipped her tea and smiled wanly at Penelope. "I imagine you must be extremely disappointed in your position, Miss Lumley. You were hired to be a governess, but this is a job more fit for a zookeeper, is it not?"

All eyes turned to Penelope. She did not want to repeat her mistake of bragging about the children's accomplishments, yet she could not let Baroness Hoover's mean remark go unanswered. "I was fortunate to receive a rigorous and well-rounded education," she said, choosing her words carefully. "I hope to impart the same to my students."

"And I might hope to grow wings and fly, but that is no guarantee of it happening!" The Baroness laughed and slurped her tea.

Judge Quinzy adjusted his glasses higher on his nose. "Perhaps you are underestimating Miss Lumley's pupils, baroness. A dog can easily be taught a few tricks. Why not these three?" He watched the children carefully. "Tell me, have you studied any foreign languages yet? French? Italian? German?"

At the word "German," Alexander sat up straight. *"Wanderlust!"* he exclaimed passionately, and then grabbed a petite madeleine as his reward. One of Judge Quinzy's eyebrows arched so high, Penelope was afraid it might come loose. The Earl of Maytag was less impressed.

"Fine. He said *wanderlust*, so what? If I say *gesundheit* when someone sneezes, it hardly means I speak German," Maytag retorted.

"It's a bit much to quiz them on languages, Quinzy," Hoover added. "Ashton said when he found them they could barely speak at all. Not even English, ha!"

"English easy," Beowulf announced. "I write poem in English." He stood up as if ready to recite.

Judge Quinzy held up a hand in alarm. "Sit down, young man. Composing English poetry is hardly something to brag about. We'll have none of that."

Hoover snorted. "You're a funny fellow, Quinzy! But you have a point. Poetry and Latin, those were my most dreaded subjects at school."

The three Incorrigibles glanced at one another and exchanged secret smiles. Penelope bit her lip. What were they up to now?

Before answering, Alexander wiped the crumbs from his chin with a napkin, just as Penelope had taught him. "Latin, yes! *Cogito, ergo sum.* 'I think, therefore I am.'"

Beowulf was already grinning and bouncing up and down for his turn. "*Veni, vedi, vici*," he declared. "'I came, I saw, I conquered.'"

Hoover pounded the table and chortled, while Maytag and the baroness exchanged skeptical looks. Judge

Quinzy's eyes grew impossibly large behind his thick lenses. "Is this your doing, governess?" he murmured in a low voice. Then he turned to Cassiopeia. "Now I shall not be satisfied until I hear what you have to say. Do you speak Latin, too, like your littermates here?" He fixed the girl with a nonthreatening half smile, but his eyes looked deadly serious.

Penelope remembered the way Cassiopeia snarled at Lady Constance the previous evening and felt a flash of fear. Put on the spot like this, what would Cassiopeia do? Would she growl? Bark? Bite him in the leg?

In a clear, strong voice, Cassiopeia pronounced, "*Vado, Pluvia!*"

There was a moment of confusion at the table.

"*'Vado, Pluvia'*?"

"It is Latin, I'll grant you that. But what does it mean?"

"*Vado* is 'go,' but *Pluvia*? Isn't that rain?"

Penelope quickly covered her mouth with her hand to conceal a smile. "I believe she intends to say, 'Go, Rainbow,'" she explained. To Cassiopeia, she added, "Next time, try *pluvius arcus*, dear; the meaning is clearer." Cassiopeia, wide-eyed and innocent, merely shrugged and ate another cake.

Lady Constance chose this moment to regain

consciousness and peeked out from under her napkin. "Oh, it's shtill the party! I was dreaming we were in church, and everyone was shinging Latin hymns." She reached for a sweet and found herself staring at Cassiopeia, who was merely trying to pass the plate. "Not fair, not fair—it's *my* party and all anyone wants to talk about is these awful, awful children. The little one almost bit me yeshterday, you know," she remarked to no one in particular. "They are all unshtable, but I believe she is the most vicious of the three."

As if in answer, the room suddenly filled with a low, whining snarl, which gradually slid higher in pitch. Penelope saw each member of the table react to the noise in his or her own fashion: Cassiopeia bared her upper teeth, and the boys grew alert and bright-eyed, ready to spring. Maytag had a look of eager excitement on his face, Hoover seemed alarmed, his wife disgusted. Only Judge Quinzy remained neutral—which is to say, whatever he was thinking, he did not let it show.

The snarl grew louder and began to run up and down the scale, until it resembled the sound of a violin being tuned.

"Hooray, hooray, the musicians are here!" Lady Constance exclaimed, launching herself precariously to her feet. "Let us all shtand for the shah-teesh!"

LADY CONSTANCE WAS CORRECT, and if you have ever had the misfortunate of hearing a violinist tuning, you will understand the momentary confusion. At this cue from the musicians, all the guests rose from their tables and arranged themselves in two long lines in the center of the dance floor, men on one side, women on the other.

Penelope did the same, but in her mind it was as if her thoughts were already dancing; they kept pairing up and running off and then coming back again in new combinations, never holding still long enough for her to make sense of them. Everything was a muddle! For weeks she had toiled to get the children in tip-top shape for the party (and what a stroke of luck it was that they had spent the morning playing with Alexander's new Latin primer!). Yet it seemed Lord Fredrick had promised his friends a trio of fur-covered wolf children who did nothing but bark and howl. And the Earl of Maytag's awful remark about hunting still gnawed at her insides.

"Surely it is all some sort of dark and unfunny joke," Penelope thought, as she took her place in the line of dancers. It was the only logical explanation; she must have misunderstood the true meaning of the conversation, for she was not used to grown men jesting with one another in such a free and sportive way. After all, the teachers at Swanburne were all women, and Dr. Westminster was known for his exceptionally gentle speech; it was said he could soothe a colicky calf merely by singing "God Save the Queen" in his pleasingly low and cowlike voice.

There was a bit of difficulty in the formation of the line, for Lady Constance was dependent on Baron Hoover and the Earl of Maytag to hold her upright; without their support she quickly ended up on all fours. This predicament was made worse for Hoover when Maytag abruptly abandoned ship and seized Penelope as his partner. Beowulf and Cassiopeia made a light-footed pair, but Judge Quinzy declined to dance at all, saying, "At my age I much prefer being a spectator. I will take a walk in the air to refresh myself while you young people enjoy these revels."

"Schottische?" Alexander asked Baroness Hoover, gallantly offering his arm. After a pitying glance at her husband, she accepted.

Soon all the guests had taken partners, and the musicians struck up the tune. As she began to move, Penelope realized that Margaret and Jasper had been right: When it came to dancing, music made all the difference. She found it a sweet relief to skip merrily around the room and let go of her nagging suspicion that something nefarious was going on. How foolish it was to worry and assume the worst—it was Christmas, after all!

The children also seemed to be enjoying themselves, and they remembered all their steps and turns perfectly. The only glitch in the whole affair was during the portions of the music when the ladies changed partners, for at each successive pairing a new gentleman would nearly stumble to the ground before realizing that his role would be not merely to partner, but to actually carry Lady Constance through the dance. The lady herself was having a conspicuously marvelous time. She kept crying out, "Oh, I feel light as a feather! I can barely feel the floor beneath my feet! If only my Fredrick were here to see," and other blurry exclamations of that sort.

In short, the schottische was a success, and it went on for a good long while. Soon everyone was warm from exertion. Someone called for a window to be opened and cool air let in. At last the musicians took their break, and the guests returned to their tables for refreshments, laughing and fanning themselves.

The fresh air seemed to clear Lady Constance's

mind somewhat; at the very least she regained the ability to stand upright. She rapped on her glass to get everyone's attention.

"Marvelous dancing, everyone! Our next entertainment will delight you just as much, I'm sure," she said. "Behold, the astonishingly lifelike *tableaux vivant* of Leeds' Thespians on Demand!"

The applause was vigorous, for, in fact, Leeds was a very well-known company. Only now did Penelope notice that, during the dancing, a curtained playing area had been quickly set up on one side of the ballroom, between the tall windows. As the applause peaked, the principal actor stepped in front of the curtain.

"Lords and ladies, on behalf of my fellow thespians, allow me to wish a happy Christmas to one and all. May I present: our first *tableau.*" With a grand gesture he pulled the curtain open.

(A brief aside: Although they have fallen out of style, in Miss Penelope Lumley's day *tableaux vivant* were all the rage. Using costumes, sets, and props, the participants arranged themselves to depict some recognizable scene—a famous painting, perhaps, or a well-known fable. No doubt this will sound dull to the modern viewer whose tastes have been shaped by more advanced forms of entertainment featuring zombies and so forth, but rest assured: The power of a well-executed *tableau* to shock and delight the audiences of its time must not be underestimated.)

A collective gasp of appreciation rose from the guests. Before them was a forest, or rather a painted backdrop of a forest, but a convincing one. Two near-naked youths clung to each other. Looming above them was a fully occupied wolf costume of the sort where one person inhabits the head of the wolf and another works the hind end. As you might imagine, it was quite a bit larger than life.

"I know it already! It's Romulus and Remus, the twins who were raised by a wolf," Baron Hoover crowed. "An apt choice, *har har har!*"

Quickly, Penelope looked to see if the children were disturbed by the scene. On the contrary, they were quite transfixed. Beowulf had a dreamy smile on his face, and Cassiopeia extended one hand as if she would pet the somewhat implausible creature before her.

"Draw the curtain, please!" Lady Constance was suddenly agitated. "That is not well-suited to my party. Show us something else."

The principal actor bowed; if he was annoyed, he hid it well. "As you wish. We have also prepared a *tableau* based on Aesop's well-loved fable 'The Boy Who Cried Wolf.'"

"Nooooo!" The word came out sounding like a growl, and Lady Constance stamped her feet in anger. "I have heard quite enough on this topic already today, I am sick to death of it! Let us not have any of these upsetting stories, if you please!"

At this point the actor playing the head of the wolf peeked out through the mouth. No doubt he was wondering at the cause of the delay. The sight of his human face inside the wolf's gullet struck the children as hilarious; all three of them burst out laughing.

"May I suggest a simple, harmless fairy tale, then?" the lead actor said, with only a touch of condescension. "Something even a child would enjoy?"

Lady Constance nodded her consent. The curtain was closed for a moment while the actors prepared. Then it was drawn open once more.

A different, more ominous-looking forest backdrop had been unfurled, and an actor dressed as a young girl in red cape and hood entered, carrying a basket. She took an innocent pose, one hand delicately framing her face. And then, emerging from the shadows, still terrifyingly larger than life, and this time with teeth bared, came the big—bad—

"No!" Lady Constance barked. "*No no no no—*"

The actor playing the head of the wolf howled.

Alexander—who could blame him?—howled along.

Beowulf, not to be outdone, howled, too.

"Now that's what we came to see," Maytag remarked to Hoover. He sounded very pleased. "That's what Ashton promised."

Cassiopeia jumped onto the foot of the stage area, threw back her head, and—

"Enough!" Lady Constance marched up to the stage and pulled the curtain shut. Then she spoke to the proprietor in a fury. "Sir! These are not the *tableaux* I instructed you to prepare. I asked for something uplifting! Something with artistic merit! And all you have to show us is wolves, wolves, and more wolves! Why is that, pray tell?"

The actor bowed his head. "I apologize, my lady, but it was specifically requested. I have it in writing."

He then reached into an interior pocket of his waistcoat and produced a letter, which he handed to Lady Constance. Her expression did not change as she read it, but when she looked up, her attitude was quite transformed. "Thank you, sir," she said. "That will be all. Everyone, let us offer our thanks to the good thespians from Leeds."

The actor playing Little Red Riding Hood pushed back his hood. "All? But we have hardly performed."

"You are Leeds' Thespians on Demand, are you not?" Lady Constance hissed through her teeth. "Well, I demand that you stop. You shall be paid your full fee, but now you must go."

As the disappointed actors took down the curtain and packed up their unused props and costumes, the party guests shrugged and resumed drinking and flirting with one another's spouses, just as party guests have done since the beginning of time. But questions pirouetted around Penelope's mind faster than even the ballerinas of the Imperial Russian Ballet could have managed: Who had requested these awful stories about children and wolves? Obviously it was not Lady Constance; she seemed as dismayed by the content of the *tableaux* as Penelope was. And what had been revealed in that letter?

The children had stopped howling, and now watched the actors packing up with keen interest. For the moment they seemed more entertained than disturbed by the strange goings-on, but Penelope's sense of foreboding had returned at twice its previous level. Unexpected encounters, unsettling remarks, a distraught hostess, a theatrical flop—the party had turned out to be much more interesting than expected, to be sure, but fresh mysteries kept slithering to the surface like earthworms after a heavy rain, and Penelope had had enough. In another few moments, she decided, she would fashion some excuse for her and the children to leave.

But, alas and alack! Timing is everything, as one of the actors from Leeds could surely have told her. If only she had reached this conclusion a few moments earlier! For at that very second a disagreement broke out between Baroness Hoover and her husband:

"We shall catch a play in London, dear. Will that make it all right?" he soothed.

"But I was so looking forward to the *tableaux*!"

"It was frightening the children, precious. Didn't you hear them howling?"

"They didn't look frightened to me," she snapped. "They looked rather at home in those tales, in fact. But if the children did not care for the actors' *tableaux*," she added slyly, "perhaps they will show us one of their own."

Then Judge Quinzy, who had returned to the party with the faintest dusting of snowflakes on his jet-black hair, turned to the Incorrigibles. "What a splendid idea," he said in his smooth, charming way. "Will you indulge the baroness and grace us with a presentation of your own choosing?"

The children were excited by the request and quickly conferred with one another in that private, guttural code they sometimes used among themselves. Penelope wondered what on earth they could be thinking of. But as she was about to discover, their thinking was not on earth. In fact, it was all at sea.

"Incorrigibles *tableaux*!" Alexander announced proudly, after another brief huddle. "Title: 'Wreck of the Hespawoo.' A poem by Longfelloo."

"Longfelloo? I think they're talking gibberish," someone griped, but he was quickly shushed by the other guests.

Using the long drawstring of her reticule as rope, Cassiopeia lashed herself firmly to a potted fern. "Mast!" she explained.

Beowulf took the role of her desperate sea captain father, while Alexander ran about them as the storm, howling like the wind, and quite convincingly, too.

"Rain!" Cassiopeia instructed. Beowulf grabbed one glass of champagne after another off a nearby serving tray and tossed them at her, until her dress was sopping and her hair dripped in wet tendrils.

"Snow, snow!" she yelled. Beowulf seized handfuls

of white linen napkins, quickly shredded them with his teeth, and flung them in the air around her. Meanwhile, Alexander seized the round silver serving tray and held it in front of him as if were the helm of the ship. Bracing himself wide and bowlegged in a way that was thrillingly reminiscent of a sea captain, he proclaimed:

"And fast through the midnight dark and drear,
Through the whistling sleet and snow,
Like a sheeted ghost, the vessel swept
Tow'rds the reef of Norman's Woe."

"Woe!" The children rocked back and forth to simulate the tossing of the ship in a storm and howled with merry abandon. "Woe-wooooe! *Awhooooooooooooooooooe!"*

"Stop them! Somebody stop them!" Lady Constance shrieked, clutching at her temples. "They are mad! Oh, my head hurts!"

"Bravo, bravo!" Baron Hoover was on his feet, applauding. "This is marvelous!"

"Children, well done, but that is enough—" Penelope was also impressed with the presentation, but she thought it best to end there. After all, it was well past

"Woe-wooooe! Awhoooooooooooooooooooe!"

bedtime, and it had been a very long day, and—

"*Eeeeeek!*" It was the lady with the fur-collared dress. She stared in horror at the floor. "*Eeeeeeeek!*" she screamed, twice as loudly. "It is alive! I think it is a rat!"

The napkin storm abated, the Hesperus stopped sinking, and everyone looked down. Something furry and trembling peeked out from beneath the edge of the woman's gown. For a sickening moment Penelope thought that the dead creatures draped around her neck had miraculously come to life and were now seeking some kind of awful revenge.

"Ashton always keeps a gun in his study," one of the men offered. "I will go—"

"No!" Penelope cried. "It is only a squirrel; they are harmless. Let me coax it to safety—"

But the *eeeeek*ing woman could not wait; she lifted the skirt of her gown and delivered a swift kick, which sent the squirrel skidding to the center of the ballroom. After giving itself a shake, it scampered in confused zigzags around the dance floor. Finally, it sat up on its haunches, its button eyes fearfully darting around, wringing its tiny monkeylike hands in dismay.

Ever sympathetic to animals in need (and urgently aware that the sooner the squirrel was whisked out of sight, the better), Penelope slowly approached. She offered the squirrel a morsel of petite madeleine. "Here, poor nubbin, now we will just lead you out of doors again where you belong—"

Before she could say more, a terrible growling sound filled the room.

It was not the violinist tuning this time. A whole army of incompetent cellists could not have made this sound. It was fierce. It was bloodcurdling. It was coming from the Incorrigibles.

Penelope wheeled around. "No," she warned in a panic. "Children, no! Squirrels no! You know better. You must calm yourselves—"

But it could not be helped. The excitement of the party, the provocation of the *tableaux*, "The Wreck of the Hesperus," the consumption of far too many sweets—the children were, as they say nowadays, over-stimulated. This was simply the squirrel that broke the camel's back. Before Penelope or anyone else could stop them, they stared, hunkered down, and pounced.

The squirrel bolted, with the children barking and yapping in pursuit. Around the ballroom the creature raced, underneath tables and up across the window ledges, although it dimwittedly ignored the one that had been opened. Soon the children had it backed into one end of the room. After a moment of terrified squeaking, it spotted the Christmas tree and jumped. Alexander leaped after it. Amid the alarmed cries of the guests, the tree swayed drunkenly, first this way, then that, before toppling over with a mighty crash.

Broken ornaments littered the floor. The women screamed; many of the men screamed also. The delicate sensibilities of Leeds' Thespians could not endure this ruckus. They clambered on top of the chairs and began declaiming, in their trained and resonant voices, an impressive variety of off-color phrases that are not necessary to reprint here.

Meanwhile, the chase continued. The squirrel maneuvered so quickly, it was nothing but a gray blur. Cassiopeia's champagne-soaked dress was badly torn; the boys' sailor suits were covered with stains and their straw hats all frayed. However, the children did look as if they were having a marvelous time.

After what seemed an eternity but was obviously not (in fact, calling any length of time "an eternity" is yet another example of hyperbole in action), the children succeeded in cornering the squirrel near the doors that led out of the ballroom. Then, in what was either a brilliant stroke of luck or a bit of disastrously poor timing, depending on whether you were rooting for the squirrel or the children, the doors swung open.

"My word!" exclaimed Mrs. Clarke. She stood in the doorway, holding a large pitcher on a tray. "I just ran downstairs to get more milk for the tea, and on the way back I heard the most terrible racket—*Aaaaaaah!* Dear heavens above, what has happened in here? It's like a hurricane hit!"

Somewhere in its nut-sized brain, the squirrel must have recognized its only chance for escape. With a desperate lash of its tail the rodent bolted between Mrs. Clarke's legs, through the doors of the ballroom, and disappeared into the vast house beyond.

The children froze, but only for a moment. Then Cassiopeia raised her tiny fists in the air. "Mayhem!" she bellowed, pointing out the door.

Spurred on by her battle cry, the yapping Incorrigibles tore off after the squirrel, in hot and, it must be said, happy pursuit.

THE FOURTEENTH CHAPTER

*In the wake of mayhem,
a disturbing discovery!*

A TRAUMATIZED HUSH fell over the party guests, punctuated only by the fizz of candles extinguishing themselves in the spilled wine that now spread in scarlet puddles over the recently scrubbed wood floors, and by the hiccupping sobs of Lady Constance. A more complete vision of chaos would be hard to imagine.

"Well," laughed one of the male guests, after what seemed like (yet obviously was not) another eternity. "I'd say the Hesperus has been well and truly wreck'd at last!"

Then the floodgates opened. The shocked silence gave way to a roar of complaints: "Look, my shoes are destroyed—and I bought them in Paris!" "Has anyone seen my spectacles?" "What sort of poorly run household would keep squirrels as pets?" And, most chilling of all to Penelope's ears: "Those awful children! No doubt they will be sent to the workhouse after this. They are not fit to live among civilized society!" She thought it was the baroness's voice, but it was hard to know. Everything was madness and misery and people shouting at one another.

"Oh, where is Fredrick?" Lady Constance had crawled atop the piano for safety. "Where is he, where is he? He has missed the party, and now everything is ruined, ruined, *ruuuuuuuuuuuuined*!" Alas, it would be inaccurate to call her outburst anything but a howl of dismay.

Penelope struggled through the crowd to get to the door, her mind fixed on a single idea: She had to find the children! She knew if she could reason with them for a moment and perhaps offer some tempting biscuits and a soothing, gentle story, they would soon regain their composure and let the squirrel go in peace (assuming there was still an intact squirrel left to set free, of course).

"Look outside—an intruder!" It was not clear who gave the warning, but a fresh chorus of screaming and weeping rose up as many frightened heads turned toward the window.

An intruder? Had the bandits come at last? Penelope was so overwrought, she was not thinking clearly. "What if the children were only trying to herd the squirrel out-doors?" she wondered frantically. "They may be outside this minute—they could be in terrible danger!"

Although she had nearly reached the door, now she turned and fought her back way through the crowd, toward the windows. Under normal circumstances Penel-ope was a stickler for good manners, but there was no way to get through without some pushing and elbowing, and her "Excuse me!" and "May I please get through?" went unheard in the hubbub. With some regret Penel-ope did what she had to do to reach the windows. When she arrived, she discovered that the ragged breathing of more than two hundred hysterical guests had fogged the glass. She had to rub a circle in it to see out.

Through that circle she saw—no, not the children—it was a ghost! "'A sheeted ghost'!" she croaked in horror. (As you no doubt recall, "sheeted ghost" was Longfellow's evocative phrase. Penelope had not got-ten a clear-enough look to see if this ghost was, in fact, wearing a sheet, or some other ghostly garb more suit-able to the weather. However, the expression was fresh in her mind, and out of her mouth it flew.)

Now, you may think it silly for a person already fifteen years of age to believe in ghosts, but Penelope had once heard a very frightening Christmas story with ghosts in it, and it had affected her thinking on the subject. It was by a rather popular writer named Mr. Dickens, who lived in London and published stories in the magazines. Miss Charlotte Mortimer had sometimes cut them out to read to the girls.

When Penelope saw the pale, wizened face in the darkness just outside the window, where no face had any business being—why, she recognized it at once! It was the very specter Mr. Dickens had described, the one who had spooked her so thoroughly that she could not bear to finish hearing the tale, even though Miss Mortimer had assured her it ended happily, with much laughter and a prize turkey fully twice the size of Tiny Tim.

"It is the ghost!" she screeched in terror. "The Ghost of Christmas Yet to Come!"

But it was not that ghost nor any other: A second rub of the fogged glass revealed it was Old Timothy, the coachman. Penelope quickly saw her mistake. Luckily, no one had paid attention to her panicked screech, as it was merely one among many, but the revelation filled her with fresh dread: Why was Old Timothy at the window? Had the pandemonium in the ballroom roused his curiosity enough to scale the hedge and look inside? Or was there some other, more sinister reason for his unexpected presence in the shrubbery?

She rapped on the windowpane, hard enough to rattle it. "Did you set a squirrel loose in the house?" she demanded to know. Conveniently, the enigmatic coachman could not hear her, since she was on one side of the glass and he was on the other, but their eyes met for the briefest second before he slipped away into the moon-cast shadows. In that second she was sure she had her answer: Old Timothy was the culprit! What other explanation could there be?

Mrs. Clarke appeared at her side drenched with milk, for the pitcher had been upended when the squirrel made its dramatic exit. "Miss Lumley! There you are," she huffed. "You must go find the children. I don't like the way some of the gentlemen are talking. Stop staring out the window like that, dear! Heavens, you look like you just saw a ghost!"

"But why would the coachman do such a thing?" Penelope felt the urge to weep welling up inside her. "Why set a squirrel loose—when he knows how the children can barely control themselves—unless he wanted them to—unless he *intended* them to . . ." She could not make enough sense of it all even to finish her own thought.

Mrs. Clarke dragged Penelope away from the window. "Calm down, dear. It's no wonder a squirrel got in. There's a window open—and look at all the trees that have been brought in the house! The poor squirrelykins couldn't tell indoors from out, that's all. Now pull yourself together, for if you don't find the children soon, the gentlemen are going to form a search party."

Whatever else Mrs. Clarke intended to say was drowned out by the rising wail of a most unpleasant sound—high-pitched, unhinged, emanating from the vicinity of the piano yet entirely unmusical.

"Find those Incorrigibles!" Lady Constance screamed. "They are running amok!"

As YOU MAY KNOW, the phrase *running amok* originally referred to elephants that had become separated from their herds and went galumphing through local villages, causing wreckage, destruction, and miscellaneous (to use Cassiopeia's term) mayhem.

Whether three small- to medium-sized children and one tiny, terrified squirrel could cut a swath of destruction comparable to that of an enraged elephant remained to be seen. Perhaps Lady Constance was guilty of hyperbole when she said the children were

"Find those Incorrigibles! They are running amok!"

"running amok," or perhaps she was offering an accurate assessment of the situation. No matter. Penelope fully intended to find the children, although she was far more worried about them (and, to a lesser but real extent, the squirrel) than she was about the antique furniture or the precious hand-loomed Arabian carpets that Lady Constance was so frantic about.

She instructed Mrs. Clarke to tell the servants not to run about the house yelling for the children (so as not to frighten them into hiding). Then her search began. There was a scattered trail of cookie crumbs to follow for a while, but it disappeared at the foot of the great central staircase. If only the children had not been so thorough in the use of their napkins!

But now was no time for regrets. She had to decide which way to go: upstairs, downstairs, or down the opposite hall to the other side of the house? "The children will be following the squirrel, that is the key," Penelope mused, which led her to the intriguing question: If Penelope were a squirrel, where would she run? (Although admittedly intriguing, the question was also nonsensical. Obviously, if Penelope were a squirrel, it would be a highly unusual squirrel. It would be a Swanburne squirrel through and through, and, therefore, its behavior could not be considered representative of the high-strung and woefully undereducated furball that is more typical of the species. But Penelope was too flustered to think of this at the time.)

"Up," she decided with conviction. "It is a squirrel's instinct to race up the trees when threatened. I have seen them do it a hundred times. I will continue my search by heading upstairs. Surely there will be some sign that the chase has gone by. I will soon pick up the trail." She did not know what exactly she expected "some sign" to be. Truthfully, she was afraid to imagine the scope of destruction the children might have left in their wake.

She was right to be afraid. The stairs themselves seemed more or less unharmed, save for some carpets kicked askew and the ribbon bows untied and thrown everywhere, but the second floor landing was, as they say nowadays, trashed. Paintings had been ripped from their frames. A chunk of plaster had been clawed or kicked out of the wall, with a long network of cracks emanating from the spot. A large vase of cut pussy willow stalks had been tipped over and shattered, with shards of broken crockery and stray catkins everywhere.

Still, Penelope convinced herself that the havoc trended in one direction slightly more so than in the other. Soon she found herself nearing Lord Fredrick's study. "If the squirrel were clever, it would hide among the taxidermy and hold very still, as if stuffed," she thought. Of course squirrels were not known for being clever; the crafty notion of using camouflage to hide in plain sight was more the kind of thing that, say, Edith-Anne Pevington would have thought of, and in fact, she had thought of it in the plot of *Too Many Rainbows*. That was the tale in which Edith-Anne had dusted a whole herd of ponies with cornstarch so that gray-dappled Rainbow could go unnoticed among them and thus escape the clutches of Barnabus Bailey, a wicked circus owner who longed to steal the talented pony for his own greedy purposes.

Penelope knew it was unlikely that any squirrel would possess even a fraction of Edith-Anne's resourcefulness, and this one in particular had already shown signs of muddled thinking. Nevertheless, she thought she ought to take a peek in the study just in case, for, as Agatha Swanburne once said, "You'll find it in the last place you look, so, for heaven's sake, keep looking until you find it!"

As she came nearer, she heard voices—men's voices—in animated discussion. She knew better than to eavesdrop, yet once more it simply could not be helped, for the voices rang out strong and clear.

"Is all this weaponry really necessary?" It was Baron Hoover.

"It's only self-defense!" the Earl of Maytag snorted. "I heard Lady Ashton say the little one bites."

Penelope froze. Mrs. Clarke had said something about a "search party"—surely they meant to search and not to hunt?

She knew it was urgent that she find the children, but now she felt it was equally important to know what the gentlemen (if one could still call them that) were planning to do. Putting aside her qualms about eavesdropping, she crept close enough to the door that she could hear every scrap of the conversation within, and listened.

"Good point. I'd prefer not to be bitten, personally. Look at this old musket! Ashton's got quite a collection here."

"We'll find them easily in this moon. It's like daylight outside. I've never seen a moon so full. And where in blazes is Ashton? He's missing all the fun."

"They're fakes! Probably just three strays he nabbed from an orphanage. I'll wager he promised them new shoes and some candy if they'd bay at the moon in front of his friends and then make themselves scarce."

"I'm not as sure as you, Maytag. What do you say, Quinzy?"

The Judge's mellifluous voice replied, "I have reason to believe Ashton did find these three in the woods. To me the more interesting question is whether they are more rightly considered animals or human. What do you gentlemen think?"

"I say animals. Strays are strays." There was a whirr and clunk, like metal grinding against metal.

"Animals who speak Latin? Preposterous. Careful, Maytag, there may be bullets in there."

"A parrot can be taught phrases in Latin. It proves nothing."

"Maytag, I say, watch where you point that—"

"As the newest member of our club, Judge Quinzy should get the last word! What is the verdict, your honor?"

There was a brief pause before Quinzy answered, "I say the Earl of Maytag has a point. If a creature that looks like a dog speaks to you in perfect Latin, you would be hard-pressed to argue that it was merely a dog, agreed? Likewise, if a creature that looks like a child comes to you howling and barking and threatening to bite, you would be perfectly justified in assuming it was not precisely a child."

"Well, that's something to bear in mind if one of them attacks." Maytag sounded quite pleased. "Can't believe Ashton's not here. He'd love this."

"I think he's pulling a joke on all of us, or trying to."

"Always a joker, that Ashton. He was the same when we were at Eton. You daren't turn your back on him for a minute, or you'd end up with a 'kick me' sign pinned to your back. We're not so easily fooled now, though, eh?"

"Not now, no, *har har!*"

Penelope scrunched her eyes shut. All her attention was focused on what she could hear. Laughter, the slapping of backs. The snakelike hiss of cold metal being rubbed with a polishing cloth. The grind and thunk of guns being loaded.

Without thinking, Penelope hurled herself into the study. She stood there, breathing hard and trying not to scream at the sight of all the guns. The men stared at her.

"The children," she panted. "They have run out into the woods. Mrs. Clarke said you might help look for them." It was a lie. She was quite convinced the children had gone upstairs, but she wanted these men as far away from them as possible, and it was easy for her to look desperate and afraid, for that is exactly how she felt. "They are very skilled at covering their tracks," she added quickly, "even in the snow. You will not have an easy time finding them—but please—if you could try—I know you are skilled hunters—"

"We will do our best," Baron Hoover said warmly.

"We'll bring 'em back, one way or another," Maytag added with a dark chuckle.

Penelope nodded and backed out of the room. She could stay quiet no longer; the sob was rising in her throat. Covering her mouth with one hand, Penelope ran, as fast as she could—almost as if she were being hunted herself.

UP THE STAIRS PENELOPE RAN. Once on the third floor she thought to check the nursery; perhaps the children had lost interest in the squirrel and found their way back there. Breathless, she dashed inside. The nursery was cold and dark. No fire had been lit, and there was no sign of the children.

She threw open the window and leaned out into the night air, craning her head this way and that. The men were right. The full moon was now at its highest and the snow caught and magnified every morsel of its eerie blue glow. Although hardly as "bright as day," as Maytag had claimed, the night was as bright as a night could be.

"They are in the house, I know they are!" Penelope

said it aloud, both to convince herself and to steady her nerves. She still believed the squirrel's natural instinct would be to climb. She also knew Ashton Place possessed a fourth floor, but she had never had cause to visit it, until now.

The stair leading to the fourth floor was not a continuation of the main stairs of the house, but a smaller back staircase that rose from the far end of the third floor, where the smallest of the guest bedrooms were located. Only the servants used this stair, for the fourth floor held only servants' quarters, storage closets for linens and out-of-season clothes, sewing rooms, and so forth.

The stair was fully enclosed and pitch-dark. Why had Penelope not thought to bring a candle? If she could see, she would be able to tell whether there were four sets of tracks in the dust. As it was, all she could do was grope her way to the top, step by unseen step, and then push open the door.

She waited for her eyes to adjust, and looked around. She was not on the fourth floor at all. She was in the attic—in the dark she must have missed the landing and gone up two flights instead of one. The ceiling was low and angled, but moonlight streamed in from a high window covered by slatted shutters at the far end of the hall, and there was just enough light to see.

As soon as she closed the stairway door behind her, she heard sounds.

Scuffling. Panting. A low, anxious whine.

And—how her heart sank to hear it!—the unmistakable sound of gnawing.

"Children?" she called in a trembling voice. "It is Miss Lumley. Where are you? Please answer me!"

"Lumawoooooo! Lumawoooooo!"

She ran in the direction of the voices, racing blindly across the rough wood floor until she skidded to a stop at the end of the passageway. There was a windowed alcove hung with heavy drapes all around, but the drape on one side had been pulled back to reveal a small landing and a short series of steps that seemed to dead-end into the wall. Beowulf was standing on the top step, Alexander on the one below.

Alexander turned to face her. His face—his mouth, to be precise—was stained crimson. So were his fingers.

"No, oh no!" she cried. "Oh, dear, I know it is not really your fault, but children—that poor, poor squirrel!"

Chatter, chatter, chatter. Penelope wheeled to the source of the sound and stared into the darkness until her eyes adjusted. In a tiny window seat, tucked low in the alcove so that it was set deep in shadow, sat Cassiopeia. In her lap was the squirrel. It chattered excitedly as Cassiopeia fed it petites madeleines out of her reticule. Evidently, she had stuffed the tiny purse full of cakes when no one was looking.

"Cassawoof new pet," Cassiopeia said happily. "I name Nutsawoo. I love." Gently, she scratched the squirrel between the ears. There was much happy chirruping in answer. "My Rainbow," she explained, gazing up at Penelope with soft, trusting eyes.

Penelope felt herself flooded with a mixture of shock, relief, confusion, and fear, for even as Cassiopeia spoke, there was a thunder of hoofbeats from below. The search party was out in force, guns loaded, galloping into the woods. They would not find the Incorrigibles there, but by the time they realized that and returned to the house, who knew what fate they might have decided for the children?

With so many emotions to sort through, it is no wonder that the only thing Penelope could manage to say was, "That is all very well, Cassiopeia—but Alexander! Beowulf! Whatever have you got smeared on your hands and faces?"

The boys' hands flew up to their mouths. They looked at each other and grinned.

"We eat the wall," Alexander explained.

"Taste bad," Beowulf added, spitting a little.

Only then did Penelope see what was behind them. The wall at the top of this strange staircase was plastered over with many layers of wallpaper. Judging from the piles of soggy, chewed-up scraps that littered the steps, the boys had been gnawing their way through each one. The top layer (that is, the most recent one) was a loud floral pattern in bright red—the dye from this is what had stained the boys' mouths crimson. Underneath that was a tasteful multicolor stripe.

But Penelope was in no mood to think about the evolution of interior design trends. "This is a frightful mess you have made!" she said sternly to the boys. "Why on earth are you tearing away at the wallpaper like that?"

"Make a hole. Someone inside," Alexander explained. He gestured for her to come up the stairs. "Listen."

"I don't hear anything," she said nervously. "And please, stop putting your mouths to the wallpaper. It looks frightful, and I am sure it is quite unsanitary."

Obligingly, Alexander and Beowulf attacked the striped layer of wallpaper by shoving their fingers under the edge of the seam. With a nod, Alexander cued his brother to pull. The paper peeled off in a whole sheet, slowly, with a long *ffffft* sound, as the ancient dried paste reluctantly turned to dust.

"Make a hole. Someone inside," Alexander explained.

But there was yet another layer underneath, or perhaps it was some kind of mural, or a large painting. Even as Penelope looked, a cloud passed over the moon and the light was snuffed out. She could only catch a glimpse—it was a dark, woodland scene—something frightened and pale in the foreground—the glint of a ravenous yellow eye—a spatter of crimson—

In the dark, Alexander pressed his ear against the wall.

"Listen," he insisted.

Penelope came closer and listened. Wait—was there something? A faint snuffling and then some guttural noises like a growl or bark, followed by a low and plaintive howl?

Ahwoooooooooooooo . . .

No. There was no howl, no sound at all; she was imagining it. In any case, it was very dark now, and she was suddenly groggy with exhaustion and freezing cold. She had had enough excitement for one day and longed for a warm fire and an interesting book. "Children," she said, shivering. "That is enough of that. We must leave at once."

"Someone, Lumawoo," Beowulf insisted. He sniffed at the wallpaper. "Someone inside."

"I am sure there is not," she said firmly. "Now we

must return to the nursery. We are all very tired, and it is far too easy to start imagining things when one is worn out. Christmas is over. It is time to go to bed—after scrubbing your faces and hands, of course."

Obediently, the boys turned away from the wall. Cassiopeia tugged at her sleeve. "My Nutsawoo? Keep?"

Penelope sighed. "He will not be happy living indoors, but he can live in the tree outside the nursery windows." Cassiopeia was content with that solution, but Penelope had to bite her lip not to comment as the little girl explained its new living situation to the attentively chirruping squirrel. Then, with her brothers' help (Beowulf had to hoist her onto Alexander's shoulders to reach), she opened the high window just enough to let creature out and closed it after.

"Nutsawoo meet us downstairs," Cassiopeia explained, jumping lightly to the floor. With deep satisfaction, she wiped her filthy hands on the shredded remains of her party dress. "Now"—*yawn!*—"Cassawoof go to bed."

The Fifteenth and Final Chapter

Lord Fredrick demands a lozenge, and the children's fate is decided.

In England (and in some other countries as well), the day after Christmas is called Boxing Day.

Nowadays, Boxing Day is the day in which stores put all their merchandise on sale, thus giving exhausted and bankrupt shoppers the chance to stand in line for hours in hopes of saving ten percent on a new microwave oven, which, presumably, would come in a box. In Miss Penelope Lumley's day it was the occasion for small boxes of holiday presents to be distributed to the servants, and that is where the name "Boxing Day" originated. In fact, on Boxing Day it was customary to give the servants the day off, and most household employees considered this the greatest gift of all.

Perhaps Lady Constance had secretly planned to declare Boxing Day a day off for the servants of Ashton Place. She had not mentioned her intention to do so, but every member of the staff, from Mrs. Clarke down the youngest stable boy, had lived in hope. In fact, Margaret and Jasper had been seen whispering plans to go ice skating on the lake should a few hours of freedom tumble unexpectedly into their laps.

But when the sun finally dared to rise on this particular Boxing Day morning, all such hopes were dashed. Lady Constance's Christmas party had ended in such a free-for-all of destruction that a whole fleet of servants working 'round the clock for a month would be hard-pressed to put the house right. There would be no day off, and if any Christmas boxes had been prepared for the staff, they were nowhere in evidence.

At least the staff had no houseguests to take care of. Once the children had charged out of the ballroom in pursuit of Nutsawoo (and you may think of that mischievous scamp as Nutsawoo from this point forward, now that he has been given a name), the party never recovered. Most of the guests insisted on leaving at once, and the few remaining stragglers had departed at daybreak without even waiting for breakfast.

Mrs. Clarke had the heartbreaking task of writing a full inventory of the damage; by half past nine in the morning, her hand was already starting to cramp. Carpets throughout the house had been flipped over and torn. Potted plants had been knocked to the ground, and the dirt spilled everywhere. Floorboards had been yanked up, and curtains had been pulled down. The ballroom floor was ruined and would have to be sanded and refinished.

As for the damage to the reputation of Ashton Place and of its hostess—that was not so easily fixed.

THE ARMED GENTLEMEN on horseback had not returned until nearly sunrise. Penelope knew this because she had spent the night in the nursery. The thought of leaving the children alone while the search party was still at large had been simply unacceptable to her. She slept in the outer nursery, where she would be near the door in case anyone attempted to enter during the night, but it was the noise out the windows of the men returning that woke her. They sounded boisterous and merry, as they had in Lord Fredrick's study. She dragged herself to the window to look out; in the predawn light she saw that they had brought back an alarming amount of game—a good-sized stag with beautiful antlers, a small bear, a great horned owl, countless bags of rabbit and pheasant. . . .

After that, she slept only fitfully. When she opened her eyes again, she had to think for a moment before recalling how she had come to spend the night curled up in a toy trunk. Then she remembered everything and wished she could close the lid on top of herself and hide, at least until spring.

The children had no such anxiety. They awoke later than usual, which was understandable given their missed bedtime, but in all other respects, they behaved as if it were a normal day. Their destroyed clothes, the ruination of the party, the damage done to the ballroom and the rest of the house—none of this weighed on the minds of the Incorrigibles. Cassiopeia was overjoyed with her new pet (who, to Penelope's surprise, appeared in the tree outside the nursery window during breakfast, chattering a greeting and begging for treats), and the boys filled their morning with a game of chess, which they had been teaching themselves to play from a pamphlet that came with the set.

Penelope watched the three of them at their tasks, cheerful and innocent of any wrongdoing. She herself did not feel the children were fully to blame for what had happened. But who was? The squirrel in the ballroom might have been an accident, but taken together with those suspiciously wolfish *tableaux* and the bizarre behavior of the gentlemen from Lord Fredrick's club—surely there was more going on here than mere coincidence could explain. Someone (or some*ones*) seemed to have wanted to provoke the children into behaving like wild things.

And what of the children's insistence that someone was living behind that strange wall in the attic? That was another mystery altogether.

"To make sense of all this, I must use my powers of deduction," Penelope thought to herself. Aloud she said only, "Watch your knight, Beowulf."

(Some years later, another rather popular writer who lived for a time in London would create a detective character known for his superb powers of deduction. Penelope had never heard of Sherlock Holmes, of course, for in a fictional sense he had not been born yet, but she was a clever girl and no stranger to logic herself. That is why she realized that her powers of deduction would come in useful when trying to figure things out.)

Calmly and methodically, Penelope considered each of the possible suspects.

Lady Constance? No doubt Lady Constance would prefer the children be sent away to live elsewhere. An outburst of horrendous behavior would certainly help her argue that case to Lord Fredrick. But she had seemed sincere and determined in her ambition to have the party go well. She had argued convincingly with the Thespians that they not present the wolf-themed *tableaux*. And she was utterly distraught over the damage that had been done to the house. No, Penelope was certain; Lady Constance would rather endure a dozen wild children living in Ashton Place than risk inciting the kind of home wrecking that had transpired. But Penelope wondered once more: What had been in that letter?

Lord Fredrick? Judging from the gentlemen's remarks, Lord Fredrick had led them to expect a spectacular display of wolflike behavior from the children at the party. Perhaps his pride was at stake—yet the cost of the repairs to the house was bound to be enormous! It did not seem reasonable to incur such an expense merely to impress one's friends; although Penelope did not know Lord Fredrick well, he did seem to her to be both reasonable and cost-conscious. Moreover, Lord Fredrick had not even attended the party. How could he be the culprit when he was not there?

The Earl of Maytag? Penelope was unsure. His

obnoxious remarks about the children seemed entirely in character; the man was obnoxious on every subject. Still, he had expressed that unfortunate wish for the children to prove themselves animals so he could—Penelope went pale to think it—go hunting. "Surely he was joking!" she thought quickly, which was just as quickly followed by the nauseating suspicion that he was not. "The verdict on Maytag," she concluded grimly, "is not yet in."

And what of Old Timothy? He had no personal grudge against the children that she knew of, but, after all, he was a very enigmatic coachman. Who knew what had prompted his presence at the window? Still, of all of them Old Timothy seemed the most culpritlike, even if Penelope had no provable reason to think so.

"If only Nutsawoo could speak!" Penelope concluded with a sigh. The poor squirrel was the only creature that might be trusted to give an honest accounting of the events that had led to its untimely arrival at the party. Unfortunately, and despite Cassiopeia's rather adorable attempts to teach it polite party conversation and socially useful phrases, the squirrel was not talking.

There was a light tapping at the nursery door. Penelope assumed it was one of the serving girls come to take away the breakfast dishes, but it was not.

"Miss Lumley, good morning," Judge Quinzy said

with a half bow. "I am sorry to disturb you, but our search party last night turned up no sign of the children. I merely wanted to inquire for myself whether they had been safely found."

"Yes, of course," Penelope felt her cheeks flush. "It seems I had been mistaken. The children had not left the house at all. They were simply—hiding."

"Like hide-and-go-seek?" Judge Quinzy smiled. "How charming." His eyes quickly scanned the nursery. His inscrutable expression became even more so at the sight of the two boys playing chess and the tiny girl with a squirrel in her lap.

"I am so sorry, Judge Quinzy," Penelope said. "I seem to have sent you and the gentlemen on a wild goose chase, in the snow, no less. You must extend my apologies."

"Ha!" The judge snapped out of his reverie. "Funny you put it that way, Miss Lumley. There is nothing the gentlemen from Lord Fredrick's club like better than a wild goose chase, and although we did not find any geese last night, we did not come back empty-handed, I assure you. The gentlemen were quite satisfied." He half bowed once more. "But, forgive me, I am keeping you from your lessons. I am glad to see the children are safe. Good day, Miss Lumley."

"Good day," Penelope said, as the judge strode

noiselessly away. She closed the nursery door behind him. This time she locked it as well.

"Miss Lumley, I am afraid we have a great deal of unpleasantness to discuss. Please have a seat."

Penelope entered the sitting room, her head held high. She had known this summons would come at some point during the day, and she was only glad she had had the chance to give the children a few final lessons in geometry before Mrs. Clarke had come to fetch her. She was not nervous; in fact, Penelope fully expected Lady Constance to fire her on the spot, so she felt she might as well say what she thought. Hence, she had a lack of fear.

"I realize you must be quite disappointed in the children's behavior," Penelope began, as soon as she was settled in her chair. "Remember that I am their governess and any errors they make are more my fault than theirs. Please, Lady Constance: Regardless of what becomes of me, I must insist that you not hold the children responsible for yesterday's unfortunate—accident."

"Accident!" Lady Constance clutched the seat of her chair so tightly, her knuckles turned white. "They ruined the party and have nearly destroyed my house! In what way can that be considered an accident?"

"They were provoked," Penelope said in a cracking

voice. "In fact, I believe they may have been provoked on purpose, although for what purpose I cannot say."

Lady Constance lowered her voice and leaned forward. "It is very odd that you say so, Miss Lumley. Very odd. For that has crossed my mind as well."

Then, much to Penelope's surprise, Lady Constance produced a letter from inside her sleeve and handed it to her. It was addressed to Leeds' Thespians on Demand, to the attention of the Management.

To Whom It May Concern:

It is my understanding that Leeds' Thespians have been engaged to perform at Ashton Place on Christmas Day.

Stories with wolves and gruesome ends are specifically requested. The enclosed funds should be sufficient to guarantee your cooperation.

Disregard any other instructions you may receive.

Regards,

The letter was signed with a large, flourished *A*. It was very like the *A* that appeared on the Ashton letterhead. Penelope had seen it twice before: on the employment contract she had signed upon her arrival at the house, and also on the note Lady Constance had given her with her salary.

Penelope looked up. She was too shocked to do anything but speak bluntly. "Wolves and gruesome ends, and signed with an *A*! Does this mean it was Lord Fredrick who requested those disturbing *tableaux* and without your knowledge?"

"I don't know what it means," Lady Constance answered tremulously. "And I have not seen Lord Fredrick since lunchtime on Christmas Eve, so I cannot ask him. It is all very mysterious! And very upsetting! And it all started when Fredrick found those awful children in the woods! I do not know what is going on, Miss Lumley, but I do know I cannot bear it any longer." She snatched the letter back. "I realize this is unpleasant for both of us, but since Fredrick is not here, it must be my decision. Given all that has happened, I have no choice but to—"

There was a kind of crashing, stumbling sound just outside the sitting room. It was followed by a grunt, then a moan, and then more crashing.

"Horrors! Have the children got loose?" Lady Constance clutched at her chair again and looked as if she might scream.

Hanging onto the door to keep himself upright, Lord Fredrick himself half swung, half stumbled into the sitting room.

"Fredrick!" Lady Constance leaped to her feet.

"Wherever have you been?"

"Oh, here and there. Merry Christmas, dear! Just got home I'm afraid. Sorry to miss the party and all that. But no great loss when you think of it. Christmas comes every year, that's lucky, what?" He looked pale and tired, and he held his hand up to his face as if the soft light sifting through the sitting room curtains was blinding him. Then he let go of the door and grabbed the back of a nearby settee for support. Penelope noticed there were scratches on his neck and the backs of his hands.

"What's going on in here, then?" He squinted in Penelope's direction. "You look familiar. Blast it all, now I remember. You're the governess, are you not?"

"For the moment, yes," Penelope mumbled, staring at her shoes.

Lady Constance's expression was cool and masklike once more. "She *was* the governess, Fredrick. In fact, I was just about to fire Miss Lumley when you walked in."

"Fired! Bad luck, that. It's not easy to find work these days." Lord Fredrick yawned widely. "But I say, Constance, if Miss Lumley here goes, who will look after the Incorrigibles?"

Lady Constance wrung her hands; for some reason, it made Penelope think of Nutsawoo. "Fredrick, now that you are home, we have a great deal to discuss. Oh,

I have been waiting for your return; it has been simply awful! The Incorrigibles must be sent away. If only you had been here to see what happened last night at the party! Those wretched children are not fit to live among humans. They must be sent to the orphanage, or the workhouse, or back to the woods, I don't care—"

"They most certainly will not. Finders keepers, what?" He laughed and then winced at the volume of his own chuckle. He clutched at his head and continued speaking, much more softly. "Anyway, I don't know what you mean, Constance. I heard the party went quite well."

Lady Constance could barely whisper her reply. "Really? And from what source did you hear this?"

"That new chap at the club, Quinzy. Ran into him leaving just as I was coming in. He said it was jolly good fun. Maytag downed a bear, and Hoover took down a fourteen-point stag. Made me sorry I missed it, to tell you the truth! As for the children, they are mine. I found 'em and I shall keep 'em here at Ashton Place until I'm good and done with 'em. And they'll need someone to look after them, so you may as well leave this Lumley person exactly where she is. Unless you want to raise them yourself, what?"

Lady Constance was so choked with rage, she could not speak but merely sputtered, *Eh-eh-eh-eh.*

"That's settled, then." Lord Fredrick rubbed his temples gingerly. "Now, if you don't mind, I need a headache lozenge, and some dyspepsia tablets, and a vinegar compress, nice and cool, please. Would you ring for someone to bring them to me? But not until I leave! Don't want to risk hearing the bell. That would be agony, what?" He lurched unsteadily to the door.

"Fredrick, dear?" All at once, Lady Constance resumed speaking in her customary sweet tone, as if it were the only voice she possessed. "Do you happen to know anything about a letter?"

"A letter? Why, there's twenty-six of 'em—which one do you mean?" He chuckled, but silently this time.

"Silly. I mean, did you send a letter to Leeds' Thespians? Telling them what sort of *tableaux* to prepare?"

He looked puzzled. "Why on earth would I do that? Thespians! Waste of money if you ask me." His hand went to his head once more. "Ring for that compress, would you? I'll be in my study, resting. With any luck I'll be up and about later, after the lozenge takes effect."

"You're not thinking of going to the club, are you?" Lady Constance asked in alarm.

"Not today, dear, no. Not quite up to it, I'm afraid." But something in his voice made it seem as if he wished he were.

AFTER LORD FREDRICK LEFT, the two young women sat in silence for a moment. Then Lady Constance burst into tears.

Penelope was not without sympathy, but she was not sure what would be the proper way to express it, given that she had just narrowly escaped being fired from her job by the person she now felt obliged to comfort.

"There, there," she said tentatively. It seemed to do no harm, so she repeated it. "There, there."

Lady Constance sprang up from her seat and wiped her eyes as she paced around the room. "How can he *refuse* to realize that the children should be sent away! They are fiendish and untamed! They are entirely inconvenient! They are not even related to me. They are orphans. It is time they took up their rightful place as burdens on society! Any sane person in my position would think so. If you were me, Miss Lumley, I assure you, you would feel exactly the same."

Penelope felt tempted to point out that, if she were Lady Constance, naturally she would feel the same, for she would no longer be Penelope; therefore, the comparison was lacking in both logic and persuasive oomph. But Lady Constance was on a bit of a tear and kept talking.

"But, no, Fredrick will not hear of it. Finders keepers,

that's all he ever says on the subject. Miss Lumley, it appears I am trapped! I am stuck with the lot of you; that much is clear. We shall have to make the best of it, then." Her round doll eyes narrowed. "But if my suspicions and yours are correct, and the children were provoked on purpose, that means someone—*someone* wanted to make a fool of me by sending that letter to the thespians! And releasing that squirrel into the house! And I intend to know who it was."

"I believe I know," said Penelope eagerly. "I believe it may have been Old—"

But she stopped, for she did not know, for certain. And was it not true that Old Timothy was the most trusted servant in the household? Surely between her word and his, his would prevail.

Nor was he the only suspect; he was merely one among many, and now this letter provided fresh and strange evidence—but in whose direction did it point? Too, Penelope longed to ask about the strange staircase the children had discovered upstairs, but she did not feel it wise to confess to Lady Constance that they had wandered into the attic without permission.

Further use of her powers of deduction would have to wait. For now it was enough to know that she and the Incorrigibles would remain together at Ashton Place and that Lady Constance might serve as an unlikely ally in the task of solving this puzzle.

"Lady Constance, we are confronted with a mystery," was what Penelope finally said in answer. "It reminds me of the words of Agatha Swanburne: 'One can board one's train only after it arrives at the station. Until then, enjoy your newspaper!'"

"Enjoy your newspaper?" Lady Constance gave a little snort. "What on *earth* does that mean?"

Then Lady Constance tossed her head and stamped both her feet in impatience. It was a gesture Penelope found endearingly ponylike, and the young governess allowed herself a smile.

"It is never one hundred percent certain what the sayings of Agatha Swanburne mean," she explained gently, "but my former headmistress, Miss Charlotte Mortimer, always insists that that is part of their value. As for the one about enjoying your newspaper, I would interpret it this way: Sometimes the wisest course of action is to simply wait and see what happens next."

Her answer gave Lady Constance pause. "Well, it is difficult to argue with that," she said, after a moment. Then she went to ring for Lord Fredrick's lozenge.

Epilogue

A Letter to Miss Charlotte Mortimer

With so much to ponder, and so much tidying up to do (for of course Penelope and the children volunteered to help clean up the dreadful mess that had been made), it was nearly a week before Penelope had organized her thoughts sufficiently to write to Miss Charlotte Mortimer about this first, eventful Christmas at Ashton Place.

She and Cassiopeia were seated in the nursery near the window, where the light was good for writing and Cassiopeia could enjoy the antics of Nutsawoo playing in the branches. Alexander and Beowulf were a little ways away, reenacting the Battle of Hastings with toy soldiers, but they were doing it quietly, and everyone was content.

After wishing her a Happy New Year and inquiring how she liked the journal Penelope had sent as a gift, in quick strokes Penelope told Miss Mortimer about the unsavory *tableaux*, the unexpected letter, the uninvited squirrel, and the unthinkable hunting expedition. She decided not to mention the mysterious howling from behind the attic wall, at least not for now. The more time passed, the more she doubted she had really heard anything, and ever since the embarrassment of mistaking Old Timothy for the Ghost of Christmas Yet to Come, she had vowed not to let her imagination run so wild in the future.

She concluded her letter with her thoughts on the question of who might have let the squirrel in, and why. Then she added a postscript about how all the fuss had ended happily, for not only had she not been fired from her position and the children sent away, but the whole escapade had led to the addition of dear Nutsawoo to their lives.

You know I believe that all children should have pets if it can possibly be managed, she wrote. *I feel it is beneficial to give even the littlest children responsibility for something more helpless and in need of care than themselves. In this way selfishness is avoided, generosity is nurtured, and the heart's affections are exercised until they can bend and stretch to encompass all the world's creatures.*

Penelope signed her name and then blew on the ink to dry it before folding the letter and addressing it for the post. During the letter writing Cassiopeia had taken out her doll-sized combs and brushes and amused herself by playing with Penelope's hair, as little girls so dearly like to do, even to this very day.

"Lumawoo hair, pretty, look."

"I am not in the habit of gazing into mirrors for entertainment," Penelope said distractedly. But she was secretly pleased by the compliment. With all the hullabaloo of getting ready for the party, she had never had time to apply the herbal poultice Miss Mortimer had sent to her, but even without it she noticed how her hair seemed to be remaining in good health—perhaps it had even acquired a bit more shine in the last week or so. No doubt the abundant food at Ashton Place and fresh country air agreed with her.

"Look," Cassiopeia said again, as she brushed Penelope's hair down its full length, now about halfway down her back. "Apples." *Apples* was her current word for all things reddish. "Cassawoof apples, Luma-woo apples," she repeated.

Before Penelope could see what on earth the girl meant, Cassiopeia pulled a lock of her own auburn hair loose from its ribbon, laid it next to a lock of her teacher's, and draped them forward over Penelope's shoulder, where they could both see them intermingled. The color was identical.

"Apples," Cassiopeia said, delighted with the discovery. "Same apples!"

"Silly girl," Penelope said fondly, as she quickly twisted her hair back into its customary bun. "It is just a trick of the light I am sure. Now, let us read another chapter of *A New Friend for Rainbow*—but this time I expect you to follow along. It is time you began learning to read for yourself. . . ."

And, with little Nutsawoo nestled in Cassiopeia's lap (for he too seemed to enjoy a good story), that is just what they did.

To Be Continued . . .

Acknowledgments

Abundant thanks to my agent, Elizabeth Kaplan, who would make a superb governess, and to my remarkable editor, Donna Bray, who loves *Jane Eyre* as much as I do. They are both Swanburne girls, through and through, and I am lucky to know them.

Thanks to Alessandra Balzer, Ruta Rimas, and all the excellent people at Balzer & Bray and HarperCollins Children's Books for their support and enthusiasm. I'm especially grateful for the attentive copyediting by Kathryn Silsand and Kimberly Craskey. Special thanks to Melissa Sarver at the Elizabeth Kaplan Literary Agency for her smarts, good cheer, and unfailing professionalism.

Squealing fangirl thanks to Jon Klassen, whose illustrations are so marvelous they make me want to howl with joy.

I salute and thank the many faithful family members and friends whose patient and supportive energies help keep this writer from slipping too far down the slope, especially Beatrix, Harry, Laury, Mana, Andrew, Joe, and of course, Bob. Lil' the dog deserves a nod also, and a scratch behind the ears.

Sincere thanks to Professor Michael Oil for his useful comments, especially regarding the work of Henry Wadsworth Longfellow.

Portions of the book were written and revised during several delightful residencies at the Lasagna Cottage Writer's Sanctuary and Snack Shack; for this I am deeply grateful. (To my fellow authors: do not endeavor to apply for this residency; it is offered by invitation only and, frankly, there is not much room at the cottage. However, the lasagna is delicious.)

Maryrose Wood
April 17, 2009